the short
second life of
bree tanner

an eclipse novella

the short
second life of
bree tanner

an eclipse novella

STEPHENIE MEYER

ATOM

ATOM

First published in the United States in 2010 by Little, Brown Books
for Young Readers, an imprint of Hachette Book Group USA
First published in Great Britain in 2010 by Atom
This paperback edition published in 2012 by Atom

15

A CIP catalogue record for this book
is available from the British Library.

ISBN 978-0-349-00131-9

Printed and bound in Great Britain by
Clays Ltd, Elcograf S.p.A.

Papers used by Atom are from well-managed forests
and other responsible sources.

Atom
An imprint of
Little, Brown Book Group
Carmelite House
50 Victoria Embankment
London EC4Y 0DZ

An Hachette UK Company
www.hachette.co.uk

www.atombooks.net

For Asya Muchnick and Meghan Hibbett

⤙ ⤚

INTRODUCTION

No two writers go about things in exactly the same way. We all are inspired and motivated in different ways; we have our own reasons why some characters stay with us while others disappear into a backlog of neglected files. Personally, I've never figured out why some of my characters take on strong lives of their own, but I'm always happy when they do. Those characters are the most effortless to write, and so their stories are usually the ones that get finished.

Bree is one of those characters, and she's the chief reason why this story is now in your hands, rather than lost in the maze of forgotten folders inside my computer. (The two other reasons are named Diego and Fred.) I started thinking about Bree while I was editing *Eclipse*. Editing, not writing—when I was writing the first draft of *Eclipse*, I had first-person-perspective blinders on; anything that Bella couldn't see or hear or feel or taste or touch was irrelevant. That story was her experience only.

The next step in the editing process was to step away from Bella and see how the story flowed. My editor, Rebecca Davis, was a huge part of that process, and she had a lot of questions for me about the things Bella didn't know and how we could make the right parts of that story clearer. Because Bree is the only newborn Bella sees, Bree's was the perspective that I first gravitated toward as I considered what was going on behind the scenes. I started thinking about living in the basement with the newborns and hunting traditional vampire-style. I imagined the world as Bree understood it. And it was easy to do that. From the start Bree was very clear as a character, and some of her friends also sprang to life effortlessly. This is the way it usually works for me: I try to write a short synopsis of what is happening in some other part of the story, and I end up jotting down dialogue. In this case, instead of a synopsis, I found myself writing a day in Bree's life.

Writing Bree was the first time I'd stepped into the shoes of a narrator who was a "real" vampire—a hunter, a monster. I got to look through her red eyes at us humans; suddenly we were pathetic and weak, easy prey, of no importance whatsoever except as a tasty snack. I felt what it was like to be alone while surrounded by enemies, always on guard, never sure of anything except that her life was always in danger.

I got to submerge myself in a totally different breed of vampires: newborns. The newborn life was something I hadn't ever gotten to explore—even when Bella finally became a vampire. Bella was never a newborn like Bree was a newborn. It was exciting and dark and, ultimately, tragic. The closer I got to the inevitable end, the more I wished I'd concluded *Eclipse* just slightly differently.

I wonder how you will feel about Bree. She's such a small, seemingly trivial character in *Eclipse*. She lives for only five minutes of Bella's perspective. And yet her story is so important to an understanding of the novel. When you read the *Eclipse* scene in which Bella stares at Bree, assessing her as a possible future, did you ever think about what has brought Bree to that point in time? As Bree glares back, did you wonder what Bella and the Cullens look like to her? Probably not. But even if you did, I'll bet you never guessed her secrets.

I hope you end up caring about Bree as much as I do, though that's kind of a cruel wish. You know this: it doesn't end well for her. But at least you will know the whole story. And that no perspective is ever really trivial.

Enjoy,
Stephenie

THE NEWSPAPER HEADLINE GLARED AT ME FROM a little metal vending machine: SEATTLE UNDER SIEGE—DEATH TOLL RISES AGAIN. I hadn't seen this one yet. Some paperboy must have just restocked the machine. Lucky for him, he was nowhere around now.

Great. Riley was going to blow a gasket. I would make sure I wasn't within reach when he saw this paper. Let him rip somebody else's arm off.

I stood in the shadow behind the corner of a shabby three-story building, trying to be inconspicuous while I waited for someone to make a decision. Not wanting to meet anyone's eyes, I stared at the wall beside me instead. The ground floor of the building housed a record shop that had long since closed; the windows, lost to weather or street violence, were filled in with plywood. Over the top were apartments—empty, I guessed, since the normal sounds of sleeping humans were absent. I wasn't surprised—the place looked like it would collapse in a stiff wind. The buildings on the other side of the dark, narrow street were just as wrecked.

The normal scene for a night out on the town.

I didn't want to speak up and draw attention, but I wished somebody would decide something. I was really thirsty, and I didn't care much whether we went right or left or over the roof. I just wanted to find some unlucky people who wouldn't even have enough time to think *wrong place, wrong time*.

Unfortunately tonight Riley'd sent me out with two of the most useless vampires in existence. Riley never seemed to care who he sent out in hunting groups. Or particularly bugged when sending out the wrong people together meant fewer people coming home. Tonight I was stuck with Kevin and some blond kid whose name I didn't know. They both belonged to Raoul's gang, so it went without saying that they were stupid. And dangerous. But right now, mostly stupid.

Instead of picking a direction for our hunt, suddenly they were in the middle of an argument over whose favorite superhero would be a better hunter. The nameless blond was demonstrating his case for Spider-Man now, skittering up the brick wall of the alley while humming the cartoon theme song. I sighed in frustration. Were we ever going to hunt?

A little flicker of movement to my left caught my eye. It was the other one Riley had sent out in this hunting group, Diego. I didn't know much about him, just that he was older than most of the others. Riley's right-hand man was the word. That didn't make me like him any more than the other morons.

Diego was looking at me. He must have heard the sigh. I looked away.

Keep your head down and your mouth shut—that was the way to stay alive in Riley's crowd.

"Spider-Man is such a whiny loser," Kevin called up to the blond kid. "I'll show you how a real super-hero hunts." He grinned wide. His teeth flashed in the glare of a streetlight.

Kevin jumped into the middle of the street just as the lights from a car swung around to illuminate the cracked pavement with a blue-white gleam. He flexed his arms back, then pulled them slowly together like a pro wrestler showing off. The car came on, probably expecting him to get the hell out of the way like a normal person would. Like he *should*.

"Hulk mad!" Kevin bellowed. "Hulk . . . SMASH!"

He leaped forward to meet the car before it could brake, grabbed its front bumper, and flipped it over his head so that it struck the pavement upside down with a squeal of bending metal and shattering glass. Inside, a woman started screaming.

"Oh man," Diego said, shaking his head. He was pretty, with dark, dense, curly hair, big, wide eyes, and really full lips, but then, who wasn't pretty? Even Kevin and the rest of Raoul's morons were *pretty*. "Kevin, we're supposed to be laying low. Riley said—"

"Riley said!" Kevin mimicked in a harsh soprano. "Get a spine, Diego. Riley's not here."

Kevin sprang over the upside-down Honda and punched out the driver's side window, which had somehow stayed intact up to that point. He fished through the shattered glass and the deflating air bag for the driver.

I turned my back and held my breath, trying my hardest to hold on to the ability to think.

I couldn't watch Kevin feed. I was too thirsty for that, and I really didn't want to pick a fight with him. I so did not need to be on Raoul's hit list.

The blond kid didn't have the same issues. He

pushed off from the bricks overhead and landed lightly behind me. I heard him and Kevin snarling at each other, and then a wet tearing sound as the woman's screams cut off. Probably them ripping her in half.

I tried not to think about it. But I could feel the heat and hear the dripping behind me, and it made my throat burn so bad even though I wasn't breathing.

"I'm outta here," I heard Diego mutter.

He ducked into a crevice between the dark buildings, and I followed right on his heels. If I didn't get away from here fast, I'd be squabbling with Raoul's goons over a body that couldn't have had much blood left in it by now anyway. And then maybe I'd be the one who didn't come home.

Ugh, but my throat *burned*! I clamped my teeth together to keep from screaming in pain.

Diego darted through a trash-filled side alley, and then—when he hit the dead end—up the wall. I dug my fingers into the crevices between the bricks and hauled myself up after him.

On the rooftop, Diego took off, leaping lightly across the other roofs toward the lights shimmering off the sound. I stayed close. I was younger than he was, and therefore stronger—it was a good thing we younger ones were strongest, or we wouldn't have lived through our first week in Riley's house. I could have passed him easy, but I wanted to see where he was going, and I didn't want to have him *behind* me.

Diego didn't stop for miles; we were almost to the industrial docks. I could hear him muttering under his breath.

"Idiots! Like Riley wouldn't give us instructions for a good reason. Self-preservation, for example. Is an ounce of common sense so much to ask for?"

"Hey," I called. "Are we going to hunt anytime soon? My throat's on fire here."

Diego landed on the edge of a wide factory roof and spun around. I jumped back a few yards, on my guard, but he didn't make an aggressive move toward me.

"Yeah," he said. "I just wanted some distance between me and the lunatics."

He smiled, all friendly, and I stared at him.

This Diego guy wasn't like the others. He was kind of . . . calm, I guess was the word. Normal. Not normal now, but normal before. His eyes were a darker red than mine. He must have been around for a while, like I'd heard.

From the street below came the sounds of nighttime in a slummier part of Seattle. A few cars, music with heavy bass, a couple of people walking with nervous, fast steps, some drunk bum singing off-key in the distance.

"You're Bree, right?" Diego asked. "One of the newbies."

I didn't like that. *Newbie*. Whatever. "Yeah, I'm Bree. But I didn't come in with the last group. I'm almost three months old."

"Pretty slick for a three-monther," he said. "Not many would have been able to leave the scene of the accident like that." He said it like a compliment, like he was really impressed.

"Didn't want to mix it up with Raoul's freaks."

He nodded. "Amen, sister. Their kind ain't nothing but bad news."

Weird. Diego was weird. How he sounded like a person having a regular old conversation. No hostility, no suspicion. Like he wasn't thinking about how easy or hard it might be to kill me *right now*. He was just talking to me.

"How long have you been with Riley?" I asked curiously.

"Going on eleven months now."

"Wow! That's older than Raoul."

Diego rolled his eyes and spit venom over the edge of the building. "Yeah, I remember when Riley brought that trash in. Things just kept getting worse after that."

I was quiet for a moment, wondering if he thought everyone younger than himself was trash. Not that I cared. I didn't care what anybody thought anymore. Didn't have to. Like Riley said, I was a god now. Stronger, faster, *better*. Nobody else counted.

Then Diego whistled low under his breath.

"There we go. Just takes a little brains and patience." He pointed down and across the street.

Half-hidden around the edge of a purple-black alley, a man was cussing at a woman and slapping her while another woman watched silently. From their clothes, I guessed that it was a pimp and two of his employees.

This was what Riley had told us to do. Hunt the dregs. Take the humans that no one was going to miss, the ones who weren't headed home to a waiting family, the ones who wouldn't be reported missing.

It was the same way he chose us. Meals and gods, both coming from the dregs.

Unlike some of the others, I still did what Riley told me to do. Not because I liked him. That feeling was *long* gone. It was because what he told us sounded right. How did it make sense to call attention to the fact that a bunch of new vampires were claiming Seattle as their hunting ground? How was that going to help us?

I didn't even believe in vampires before I was

one. So if the rest of the world didn't believe in vampires, then the rest of the vampires must be hunting smart, the way Riley said to do it. They probably had a good reason.

And like Diego'd said, hunting smart just took a little brains and patience.

Of course, we all slipped up a lot, and Riley would read the papers and groan and yell at us and break stuff—like Raoul's favorite video-game system. Then Raoul would get mad and take somebody else apart and burn him up. Then Riley would be pissed off and he'd do another search to confiscate all the lighters and matches. A few rounds of this, and then Riley would bring home another handful of vampirized dregs kids to replace the ones he'd lost. It was an endless cycle.

Diego inhaled through his nose—a big, long pull—and I watched his body change. He crouched on the roof, one hand gripping the edge. All that strange friendliness disappeared, and he was a hunter.

That was something I recognized, something I was comfortable with because I understood it.

I turned off my brain. It was time to hunt. I took a deep breath, drawing in the scent of the blood inside the humans below. They weren't the only humans around, but they were the closest. *Who* you were going to hunt was the kind of decision you had to make before you scented your prey. It was too late now to choose anything.

Diego dropped from the roof edge, out of sight. The sound of his landing was too low to catch the attention of the crying prostitute, the zoned-out prostitute, or the angry pimp.

A low growl ripped from between my teeth. Mine. The blood was *mine*. The fire in my throat flared and I couldn't think of anything else.

I flipped myself off the roof, spinning across the street so that I landed right next to the crying blonde. I could feel Diego close behind me, so I growled a warning at him while I caught the surprised girl by the hair. I yanked her to the alley wall, putting my back against it. Defensive, just in case.

Then I forgot all about Diego, because I could feel the heat under her skin, hear the sound of her pulse thudding close to the surface.

She opened her mouth to scream, but my teeth crushed her windpipe before a sound could come out. There was just the gurgle of air and blood in her lungs, and the low moans I could not control.

The blood was warm and sweet. It quenched the fire in my throat, calmed the nagging, itching emptiness in my stomach. I sucked and gulped, only vaguely aware of anything else.

I heard the same noise from Diego—he had the man. The other woman was unconscious on the ground. Neither had made any noise. Diego was good.

The problem with humans was that they just never had enough blood in them. It seemed like only seconds later the girl ran dry. I rattled her limp body in frustration. Already my throat was beginning to burn again.

I threw the spent body to the ground and crouched against the wall, wondering if I could grab the unconscious girl and make off with her before Diego could catch up to me.

Diego was already finished with the man. He looked at me with an expression that I could only describe as . . . sympathetic. But I could have been dead wrong. I couldn't remember anyone ever giving me sympathy before, so I wasn't positive what it looked like.

"Go for it," he told me, nodding to the limp girl on the ground.

"Are you kidding me?"

"Naw, I'm good for now. We've got time to hunt some more tonight."

Watching him carefully for some sign of a trick, I darted forward and snagged the girl. Diego made no move to stop me. He turned away slightly and looked up at the black sky.

I sank my teeth into her neck, keeping my eyes on him. This one was even better than the last. Her blood was entirely clean. The blonde girl's blood had the bitter aftertaste that came with drugs— I was so used to that, I'd barely noticed. It was rare for me to get really clean blood, because I followed the dregs rule. Diego seemed to follow the rules, too. He must have smelled what he was giving up.

Why had he done it?

When the second body was empty, my throat felt better. There was a lot of blood in my system. I probably wouldn't really burn for a few days.

Diego was still waiting, whistling quietly through his teeth. When I let the body fall to the ground with a thud, he turned back to me and smiled.

"Um, thanks," I said.

He nodded. "You looked like you needed it more than me. I remember how hard it is in the beginning."

"Does it get easier?"

He shrugged. "In some ways."

We looked at each other for a second.

"Why don't we dump these bodies in the sound?" he suggested.

I bent down, grabbed the dead blonde, and slung her limp body over my shoulder. I was about to get the other one, but Diego was there before me, the pimp already on his back.

"I got it," he said.

I followed him up the alley wall, and then we swung across the girders under the freeway. The lights from the cars below didn't touch us. I thought how stupid people were, how oblivious, and I was glad I wasn't one of the clueless.

Hidden in the darkness, we made our way to an empty dock, closed for the night. Diego didn't hesitate at the end of the concrete, he just jumped right over the edge with his bulky burden and disappeared into the water. I slid in after him.

He swam as sleek and quick as a shark, shooting deeper and farther out into the black sound. He stopped suddenly when he found what he was looking for—a huge, slime-covered boulder on the ocean floor, sea stars and garbage clinging to its sides. We had to be more than a hundred feet deep—to a human, it would have seemed pitch-black here. Diego let go of his bodies. They swayed slowly in the current beside him while he shoved his hand into the mucky sand at the base of the rock. After a second he found a hold and ripped the boulder up from its resting spot. The weight of it drove him waist-deep into the dark seafloor.

He looked up and nodded to me.

I swam down to him, hooking his bodies with one hand on my way. I shoved the blonde into the black hole under the rock, then pushed the second girl and the pimp in after her. I kicked them lightly to make sure they were in, and then got out of the way. Diego let the boulder fall. It wobbled a little, adjusting to the newly uneven foundation. He kicked his way out of the muck, swam to the top of the boulder, and then pushed it down, grinding the obstructions flat underneath.

He swam back a few yards to view his work.

Perfect, I mouthed. These three bodies would never resurface. Riley would never hear a story about them on the news.

He grinned and held up his hand.

It took me a minute to understand that he was looking for a high five. Hesitantly, I swam forward, tapped my palm to his, then kicked away, putting some distance between us.

Diego got a weird expression on his face, and then he shot to the surface like a bullet.

I darted up after him, confused. When I broke through to the air, he was almost choking on his laughter.

"What?"

He couldn't answer me for a minute. Finally he blurted out, "Worst high five *ever*."

I sniffed, irritated. "Couldn't be sure you weren't just going to rip my arm off or something."

Diego snorted. "I wouldn't do that."

"Anyone else would," I countered.

"True, that," he agreed, suddenly not as amused. "You up for a little more hunting?"

"Do you have to ask?"

We came out of the water under a bridge and lucked right into two homeless guys sleeping in ancient, filthy sleeping bags on top of a shared mattress of old newspapers. Neither one of them woke up. Their blood was soured by alcohol, but still better than nothing. We buried them in the sound, too, under a different rock.

"Well, I'm good for a few weeks," Diego said when we were out of the water again, dripping on the end of another empty dock.

I sighed. "I guess that's the easier part, right? I'll be burning again in a couple of days. And then Riley will probably send me out with more of Raoul's mutants again."

"I can come with you, if you want. Riley pretty much lets me do what I want."

I thought about the offer, suspicious for a second. But Diego really didn't seem like any of the others. I felt different with him. Like I didn't need to watch my back so much.

"I'd like that," I admitted. It felt off to say this. Too vulnerable or something.

But Diego just said "cool" and smiled at me.

"So how come Riley gives you such a long leash?" I asked, wondering about the relationship there. The more time I spent with Diego, the less I could picture him being in tight with Riley. Diego was so . . . friendly. Nothing like Riley. But maybe it was an opposites-attract thing.

"Riley knows he can trust me to clean up my messes. Speaking of which, do you mind running a quick errand?"

I was starting to be entertained by this strange boy. Curious about him. I wanted to see what he would do.

"Sure," I said.

He bounded across the dock toward the road that ran along the waterfront. I followed after. I caught the scent of a few humans, but I knew it was too dark and we were too fast for them to see us.

He chose to travel across rooftops again. After a few jumps, I recognized both our scents. He was retracing our earlier path.

And then we were back to that first alley, where Kevin and the other guy had gotten stupid with the car.

"Unbe*liev*able," Diego growled.

Kevin and Co. had just left, it appeared. Two other cars were stacked on top of the first, and a handful of bystanders had been added to the body count. The cops weren't here yet—because anyone who might have reported the mayhem was already dead.

"Help me sort this out?" Diego asked.

"Okay."

We dropped down, and Diego quickly threw the cars into a new arrangement, so that it sort of looked like they'd hit each other rather than been piled up by a giant tantrum-throwing baby. I grabbed the two dry, lifeless bodies abandoned on the pavement and stuffed them under the apparent site of impact.

"Bad accident," I commented.

Diego grinned. He took a lighter out of a ziplock from his pocket and started igniting the clothes of the victims. I grabbed my own lighter—Riley reissued these when we went hunting; Kevin *should* have used his—and got to work on the upholstery. The bodies, dried out and laced with flammable venom, blazed up quickly.

"Get back," Diego warned, and I saw that he had the first car's gas hatch open and the lid screwed off the tank. I jumped up the closest wall, perching a story above to watch. He took a few steps back and lit a match. With perfect aim, he tossed it into the small hole. In the same second, he leaped up beside me.

The boom of the explosion shook the whole street. Lights started going on around the corner.

"Well done," I said.

"Thanks for your help. Back to Riley's?"

I frowned. Riley's house was the last place I wanted to spend the rest of my night. I didn't want to see Raoul's stupid face or listen to the constant shrieking and fighting. I didn't want to have to grit my teeth and hide out behind Freaky Fred so that people would leave me alone. And I was out of books.

"We've got some time," Diego said, reading my expression. "We don't have to go right away."

"I could use some reading material."

"And I could use some new music." He grinned. "Let's go shopping."

We moved quickly through town—over rooftops again and then darting through shadowy streets when the buildings got farther apart—to a friendlier neighborhood. It didn't take long to find a strip mall with one of the big chain bookstores. I snapped the lock on the roof access hatch and let us in. The store was empty, the only alarms on the windows and doors. I went straight to the *H*'s, while Diego headed to the music section in the back. I'd just finished with Hale. I took the next dozen books in line; that would keep me a couple of days.

I looked around for Diego and found him sitting at one of the café tables, studying the backs of his new CDs. I paused, then joined him.

This felt strange because it was familiar in a haunting, uncomfortable way. I had sat like this before—across a table from someone. I'd chatted casually with that person, thinking about things that were not life and death or thirst and blood. But that had been in a different, blurry lifetime.

The last time I'd sat at a table with someone, that someone had been Riley. It was hard to remember that night for a lot of reasons.

"So how come I never notice you around the house?" Diego asked abruptly. "Where do you hide?"

I laughed and grimaced at the same time. "I usually kick it behind wherever Freaky Fred is hanging out."

His nose wrinkled. "Seriously? How do you stand that?"

"You get used to it. It's not so bad behind him as it is in front. Anyway, it's the best hiding place I've found. Nobody gets close to Fred."

Diego nodded, still looking kind of grossed out. "That's true. It's a way to stay alive."

I shrugged.

"Did you know that Fred is one of Riley's favorites?" Diego asked.

"Really? *How?*" No one could stand Freaky Fred. I was the only one who tried, and that was solely out of self-preservation.

Diego leaned toward me conspiratorially. I was already so used to his strange way that I didn't even flinch.

"I heard him on the phone with *her.*"

I shuddered.

"I know," he said, sounding sympathetic again. Of course, it wasn't weird that we could sympathize with each other when it came to *her.* "This was a few months back. Anyway, Riley was talking about Fred, all excited. From what they were saying, I guess that some vampires can do things. More than what normal vampires can do, I mean. And that's good— something *she*'s looking for. Vampires with skillzzz."

He pulled the *Z* sound out, so I could hear how he was spelling it in his head.

"What kinds of skills?"

"All kinds of stuff, it sounds like. Mind reading and tracking and even seeing the future."

"Get out."

"I'm not kidding. I guess Fred can sort of repel people on purpose. It's all in our heads, though. He makes us repulsed at the thought of being near him."

I frowned. "How is that a good thing?"

"Keeps him alive, doesn't it? Guess it keeps you alive, too."

I nodded. "Guess so. Did he say anything about anyone else?" I tried to think of anything strange I'd seen or felt, but Fred was one of a kind. The clowns in the alley tonight pretending to be superheroes hadn't been doing anything the rest of us couldn't do.

"He talked about Raoul," Diego said, the corner of his mouth twisting down.

"What skill does Raoul have? Super-stupidity?"

Diego snorted. "Definitely that. But Riley thinks he's got some kind of magnetism—people are drawn to him, they follow him."

"Only the mentally challenged."

"Yeah, Riley mentioned that. Didn't seem to be effective on the"—he broke out a decent impression of Riley's voice—"'*tamer* kids.'"

"Tame?"

"I inferred that he meant people like us, who are able to think occasionally."

I didn't like being called tame. It didn't sound like a good thing when you put it that way. Diego's way sounded better.

"It was like there was a reason Riley needed Raoul to lead—something's coming, I think."

A weird tingle spasmed along my spine when he said that, and I sat up straighter. "Like what?"

"Do you ever think about why Riley is always after us to keep a low profile?"

I hesitated for half a second before answering. This wasn't the line of inquiry I would have expected from Riley's right-hand man. Almost like he was questioning what Riley had told us. Unless Diego was asking this *for* Riley, like a spy. Finding out what the "kids" thought of him. But it didn't feel like that. Diego's dark red eyes were open and confiding. And why would Riley care? Maybe the way the others talked about Diego wasn't based on anything real. Just gossip.

I answered him truthfully. "Yeah, actually I was *just* thinking about that."

"We aren't the only vampires in the world," Diego said solemnly.

"I know. Riley says stuff sometimes. But there can't be *too* many. I mean, wouldn't we have noticed, before?"

Diego nodded. "That's what I think, too. Which is why it's pretty weird that *she* keeps making more of us, don't you think?"

I frowned. "Huh. Because it's not like Riley actually *likes* us or anything. . . ." I paused again, waiting to see if he would contradict me. He didn't. He just waited, nodding slightly in agreement, so I continued. "And *she* hasn't even introduced herself.

You're right. I hadn't looked at it that way. Well, I hadn't really thought about it at all. But then, what do they want us *for?*"

Diego raised one eyebrow. "Wanna hear what I think?"

I nodded warily. But my anxiety had nothing to do with him now.

"Like I said, something is coming. I think *she* wants protection, and she put Riley in charge of creating the front line."

I thought this through, my spine prickling again. "Why wouldn't they tell us? Shouldn't we be, like, on the lookout or something?"

"That would make sense," he agreed.

We looked at each other in silence for a few long-seeming seconds. I had nothing more, and it didn't look like he did, either.

Finally I grimaced and said, "I don't know if I buy it—the part about Raoul being good for *anything*, that is."

Diego laughed. "Hard to argue that one." Then he glanced out the windows at the dark early morning. "Out of time. Better head back before we turn into crispies."

"Ashes, ashes, we all fall down," I sang under my breath as I got to my feet and collected my pile.

Diego chuckled.

We made one more quick stop on our way—hit the empty Target next door for big ziplocks and two backpacks. I double-bagged all my books. Water-damaged pages annoyed me.

Then we mostly roof-topped it back to the water. The sky was just faintly starting to gray up in the east. We slipped into the sound right under the noses of two oblivious night watchmen by the big ferry—good thing for them I was full or they would have been too close for my self-control—and then raced through the murky water back toward Riley's place.

At first I didn't know it was a race. I was just swimming fast because the sky was getting lighter. I didn't usually push the time like this. If I were being honest with myself, I'd pretty much turned into a huge vampire nerd. I followed the rules, I didn't cause trouble, I hung out with the most unpopular kid in the group, and I always got home early.

But then Diego really kicked it into gear. He got a few lengths ahead of me, turned back with a smile that said, *what, can't you keep up?* and then started booking it again.

Well, I wasn't taking that. I couldn't really remember if I'd been the competitive type before—it all seemed so far away and unimportant—but maybe I was, because I responded right away to the challenge. Diego was a good swimmer, but I was way stronger, especially after just feeding.

See ya, I mouthed as I passed him, but I wasn't sure he saw.

I lost him back in the dark water, and I didn't waste time looking to see by how much I was winning. I just jetted through the sound till I hit the edge of the island where the most recent of our homes was located. The last one had been a big cabin in the middle of Snowville-Nowhere on the side of some mountain in the Cascades. Like the last one, this house was remote, had a big basement, and had recently deceased owners.

I raced up onto the shallow stony beach and then dug my fingers into the sandstone bluff and flew up. I heard Diego come out of the water just as I gripped the trunk of an overhanging pine and flipped myself over the cliff edge.

Two things caught my attention as I landed gently on the balls of my feet. One: it was really light out. Two: the house was gone.

Well, not entirely gone. Some of it was still visible, but the space the house had once occupied was empty. The roof had collapsed into ragged, angular wooden lace, charred black, sagging lower than the front door had been.

The sun was rising fast. The black pine trees were showing hints of evergreen. Soon the paler tips would stand out against the dark, and at about that point I would be dead.

Or *really* dead, or whatever. This second thirsty, superhero life would go up in a sudden burst of flames. And I could only imagine that the burst would be very, very painful.

This wasn't the first time I'd seen our house destroyed—with all the fights and fires in the basements, most of them lasted only a few weeks—but it was the first time I'd come across the scene of destruction with the first faint rays of sunlight threatening.

I sucked in a gasp of shock as Diego landed beside me.

"Maybe burrow under the roof?" I whispered. "Would that be safe enough or—?"

"Don't freak out, Bree," Diego said, sounding too calm. "I know a place. C'mon."

He did a very graceful backflip off the bluff edge.

I didn't think the water would be enough of a filter to block the sun. But maybe we couldn't burn if we were submerged? It seemed like a really poor plan to me.

However, instead of tunneling under the burned-out hull of the wrecked house, I dove off the cliff behind him. I wasn't sure of my reasoning, which was a strange feeling. Usually I did what I always did—followed the routine, did what made sense.

I caught up to Diego in the water. He was racing again, but with no nonsense this time. Racing the sun.

He whipped around a point on the little island and then dove deep. I was surprised he didn't hit the rocky floor of the sound, and more surprised when I could feel the blast of warmer current flowing from what I had thought was no more than an outcropping of rock.

Smart of Diego to have a place like this. Sure, it wasn't going to be fun to sit in an underwater cavern all day—not breathing started to irritate after a few hours—but it was better than exploding into ashes. I should have been thinking like Diego was. Thinking about something other than blood, that is. I should have been prepared for the unexpected.

Diego kept going through a narrow crevice in the rocks. It was black as ink in here. Safe. I couldn't swim anymore—the space was too tight—so I scrambled through like Diego, climbing through the twisting space. I kept waiting for him to stop, but he didn't. Suddenly I realized that we really *were* going up. And then I heard Diego hit the surface.

I was out a half second after he was.

The cave was no more than a small hole, a

burrow about the size of a Volkswagen Beetle, though not as tall as that. A second crawl space led out the back, and I could taste the fresh air coming from that direction. I could see the shape of Diego's fingers repeated again and again in the texture of the limestone walls.

"Nice place," I said.

Diego smiled. "Better than Freaky Fred's backside."

"I can't argue with that. Um. Thanks."

"You're welcome."

We looked at each other in the dark for a minute. His face was smooth and calm. With anyone else, Kevin or Kristie or any of the others, this would have been terrifying—the constricted space, the forced closeness. The way I could smell his scent on every side of me. That could have meant a quick and painful death at any second. But Diego was so composed. Not like anyone else.

"How old are you?" he asked abruptly.

"Three months. I told you that."

"That's not what I meant. Um, how old *were* you? I guess that's the right way to ask."

I leaned away, uncomfortable, when I realized he was talking about *human* stuff. Nobody talked about that. Nobody wanted to think about it. But I didn't want to end the conversation, either. Just having a conversation at all was something new and different. I hesitated, and he waited with a curious expression.

"I was, um, I guess fifteen. Almost sixteen. I can't remember the day . . . was I past my birthday?" I tried to think about it, but those last hungry weeks were a big blur, and it hurt my head in a weird way to try to clear them up. I shook my head, let it go. "How about you?"

"I was just past my eighteenth," Diego said. "So close."

"Close to what?"

"Getting out," he said, but he didn't continue. There was an awkward silence for a minute, and then he changed the subject.

"You've done really well since you got here," he said, his eyes sweeping across my crossed arms, my folded legs. "You've survived—avoided the wrong kind of attention, kept intact."

I shrugged and then yanked my left t-shirt sleeve up to my shoulder so he could see the thin, ragged line that circled my arm.

"Got this ripped off once," I admitted. "Got it back before Jen could toast it. Riley showed me how to put it back on."

Diego smiled wryly and touched his right knee with one finger. His dark jeans covered the scar that must have been there. "It happens to everybody."

"Ouch," I said.

He nodded. "Seriously. But like I was saying before, you're a pretty decent vampire."

"Am I supposed to say thanks?"

"I'm just thinking out loud, trying to make sense of things."

"What things?"

He frowned a little. "What's really going on. What Riley's up to. Why he keeps bringing the most random kids to *her*. Why it doesn't seem to matter to Riley if it's someone like you or if it's someone like that idiot Kevin."

It sounded like he didn't know Riley any better than I did.

"What do you mean, someone like me?" I asked.

"You're the kind that Riley should be looking for—the smart ones—not just these stupid gang-bangers that Raoul keeps bringing in. I bet you weren't some junkie ho when you were human."

I shifted uneasily at the last word. Diego kept waiting for my answer, like he hadn't said anything weird. I took a deep breath and thought back.

"I was close enough," I admitted after a few seconds of his patient watching. "Not there yet, but in a few more weeks . . ." I shrugged. "You know, I don't remember much, but I do remember thinking there was nothing more powerful on this planet than just plain old hunger. Turns out, thirst is worst."

He laughed. "Sing it, sister."

"What about you? You weren't a troubled teen runaway like the rest of us?"

"Oh, I was troubled, all right." He stopped talking.

But I could sit around and wait for the answers to inappropriate questions, too. I just stared at him.

He sighed. The scent of his breath was nice. Everybody smelled sweet, but Diego had a little something extra—some spice like cinnamon or cloves.

"I tried to stay away from all that junk. Studied hard. I was gonna get out of the ghetto, you know. Go to college. Make something of myself. But there was a guy—not much different than Raoul. Join or die, that was his motto. I wasn't having any, so I stayed away from his group. I was careful. Stayed alive." He stopped, closing his eyes.

I wasn't done being pushy. "And?"

"My kid brother wasn't as careful."

I was about to ask if his brother had joined or died, but the expression on his face made asking unnecessary. I looked away, not sure how to respond. I couldn't really understand his loss, the pain it still clearly caused him to feel. I hadn't left anything behind that I still missed. Was that the difference? Was that why he dwelled on memories that the rest of us shunned?

I still didn't see how Riley came into this. Riley and the cheeseburger of pain. I wanted that part of the story, but now I felt bad for pushing him to answer.

Lucky for my curiosity, Diego kept going after a minute.

"I kind of lost it. Stole a gun from a friend and went hunting." He chuckled darkly. "Wasn't as good at it then. But I got the guy that got my brother before they got me. The rest of his crew had me cornered in an alley. Then, suddenly, Riley was there, between me and them. I remember thinking he was the whitest guy I'd ever seen. He didn't even look at the others when they shot him. Like the bullets were flies. You know what he said to me? He said, 'Want a new life, kid?'"

"Hah!" I laughed. "That's way better than mine. All I got was, 'Want a burger, kid?'"

I still remembered how Riley'd looked that night, though the image was all blurry because my eyes'd sucked back then. He was the hottest boy I'd ever seen, tall and blond and perfect, every feature. I knew his eyes must be just as beautiful behind the dark sunglasses he never took off. And his voice was so gentle, so kind. I figured I knew what he would want in exchange for the meal, and I would have given it to him, too. Not because he was so pretty to look at, but because I hadn't eaten anything but trash for two weeks. It turned out he wanted something else, though.

Diego laughed at the burger line. "You must have been pretty hungry."

"Damn straight."

"So why were you so hungry?"

"Because I was stupid and ran away before I had a driver's license. I couldn't get a real job, and I was a bad thief."

"What were you running from?"

I hesitated. The memories were a little more clear as I focused on them, and I wasn't sure I wanted that.

"Oh, c'mon," he coaxed. "I told you mine."

"Yeah, you did. Okay. I was running from my dad. He used to knock me around a lot. Probably did the same to my mom before she took off. I was pretty little then—I didn't know much. It got worse. I figured if I waited too long I'd end up dead. He told me if I ever ran away I'd starve. He was right about that—only thing he was ever right about as far as I'm concerned. I don't think about it much."

Diego nodded in agreement. "Hard to remember that stuff, isn't it? Everything's so fuzzy and dark."

"Like trying to see with mud in your eyes."

"Good way to put it," he complimented me. He

squinted at me like he was trying to see, and rubbed his eyes.

We laughed together again. Weird.

"I don't think I've laughed *with* anybody since I met Riley," he said, echoing my thoughts. "This is nice. *You're* nice. Not like the others. You ever try to have a conversation with one of them?"

"Nope, I haven't."

"You're not missing anything. Which is my point. Wouldn't Riley's standard of living be a little higher if he surrounded himself with decent vampires? If we're supposed to protect *her*, shouldn't he be looking for the smart ones?"

"So Riley doesn't need brains," I reasoned. "He needs numbers."

Diego pursed his lips, considering. "Like chess. He's not making knights and bishops."

"We're just pawns," I realized.

We stared at each other again for a long minute.

"I don't want to think that," Diego said.

"So what do we do?" I asked, using the plural automatically. Like we were already a team.

He thought about my question for a second, seeming uneasy, and I regretted the "we." But then he said, "What can we do when we don't know what's happening?"

So he didn't mind the team thing, which made

me feel really good in a way I didn't remember ever feeling before. "I guess we keep our eyes open, pay attention, try to figure it out."

He nodded. "We need to think about everything Riley's told us, everything he's done." He paused thoughtfully. "You know, I tried to hash some of this out with Riley once, but he couldn't have cared less. Told me to keep my mind on more important things—like thirst. Which was all I could think about then, of course. He sent me out hunting, and I stopped worrying. . . ."

I watched him thinking about Riley, his eyes unfocused as he relived the memory, and I wondered. Diego was my first friend in this life, but I wasn't his.

Suddenly his focus snapped back to me. "So what have we learned from Riley?"

I concentrated, running through the last three months in my head. "He really doesn't tell us much, you know. Just the vampire basics."

"We'll have to listen more carefully."

We sat in silence, pondering this. I mostly thought about how much I didn't know. And why hadn't I worried about everything I didn't know before now? It was like talking to Diego had cleared my head. For the first time in three months, *blood* was not the main thing in there.

The silence lasted for a while. The black hole I'd felt funneling fresh air into the cave wasn't black anymore. It was dark gray now and getting infinitesimally lighter with each second. Diego noticed me eyeing it nervously.

"Don't worry," he said. "Some dim light gets in here on sunny days. It doesn't hurt." He shrugged.

I scooted closer to the hole in the floor, where the water was disappearing as the tide went out.

"Seriously, Bree. I've been down here before during the day. I told Riley about this cave—and how it was mostly filled with water, and he said it was cool when I needed to get out of the madhouse. Anyway, do I look like I got singed?"

I hesitated, thinking about how different his relationship with Riley was than mine. His eyebrows rose, waiting for an answer. "No," I finally said. "But . . ."

"Look," he said impatiently. He crawled swiftly to the tunnel and stuck his arm in up to the shoulder. "Nothing."

I nodded once.

"Relax! Do you want me to see how high I can go?" As he spoke, he stuck his head into the hole and started climbing.

"Don't, Diego." He was already out of sight. "I'm relaxed, I swear."

He was laughing—it sounded like he was already several yards up the tunnel. I wanted to go after him, to grab his foot and yank him back, but I was frozen with stress. It would be stupid to risk my life to save some total stranger. But I hadn't had anything close to a friend in forever. Already it would be hard to go back to having no one to talk to, after only one night.

"*No estoy quemando,*" he called down, his tone teasing. "Wait . . . is that . . . ? *Ow!*"

"Diego?"

I leaped across the cave and stuck my head into the tunnel. His face was right there, inches from mine.

"Boo!"

I flinched back from his proximity—just a reflex, old habit.

"Funny," I said dryly, moving away as he slid back into the cave.

"You need to unwind, girl. I've looked into this, okay? Indirect sunlight doesn't hurt."

"So you're saying that I could just stand under a nice shady tree and be fine?"

He hesitated for a minute, as if debating whether or not to tell me something, and then said quietly, "I did once."

I stared at him, waiting for the grin. Because this was a joke.

It didn't come.

"Riley said . . . ," I started, and then my voice trailed off.

"Yeah, I know what Riley said," he agreed. "Maybe Riley doesn't know as much as he says he does."

"But Shelly and Steve. Doug and Adam. That kid with the bright red hair. All of them. They're gone because they didn't get back in time. Riley saw the ashes."

Diego's brows pulled together unhappily.

"Everyone knows that old-timey vampires had to stay in coffins during the day," I went on. "To keep out of the sun. That's common knowledge, Diego."

"You're right. All the stories do say that."

"And what would Riley gain by locking us up in a lightproof basement—one big group coffin—all day, anyway? We just demolish the place, and he has to deal with all the fighting, and it's constant turmoil. You can't tell me he enjoys it."

Something I'd said surprised him. He sat with his mouth open for a second, then closed it.

"What?"

"Common knowledge," he repeated. "What do vampires do in coffins all day?"

"Er—oh yeah, they're supposed to sleep, right? But I guess they're probably just lying there bored, 'cause we don't . . . Okay, so that part's wrong."

"Yeah. In the stories they're not just asleep, though. They're totally unconscious. They *can't* wake up. A human can walk right up and stake them, no problem. And that's another thing—stakes. You really think someone could shove a piece of wood through you?"

I shrugged. "I haven't really thought about it. I mean, not a normal piece of wood, obviously. Maybe sharpened wood has some kind of . . . I don't know. Magical properties or something."

Diego snorted. "Please."

"Well, I don't know. I wouldn't just hold still while some human ran at me with a filed broom handle, anyway."

Diego—still with a sort of disgusted look on his face, as if magic were really such a reach when you're a vampire—rolled to his knees and started clawing into the limestone above his head. Tiny stone shards filled his hair, but he ignored them.

"What are you doing?"

"Experimenting."

He dug with both hands until he could stand upright, and then kept going.

"Diego, you get to the surface, you explode. Stop it."

"I'm not trying to—ah, here we go."

There was a loud crack, and then another crack, but no light. He ducked back down to where I could see his face, with a piece of tree root in his hand, white, dead, and dry under the clumps of dirt. The edge where he'd broken it was a sharp, uneven point. He tossed it to me.

"Stake me."

I tossed it back. "Whatever."

"Seriously. You know it can't hurt me." He lobbed the wood to me; instead of catching it, I batted it back.

He snagged it out of the air and groaned. "You are so . . . *superstitious*!"

"I am a *vampire*. If that doesn't prove that superstitious people are *right*, I don't know what does."

"Fine, I'll do it."

He held the branch away from himself dramatically, arm extended, like it was a sword and he was about to impale himself.

"C'mon," I said uneasily. "This is silly."

"That's *my* point. Here goes nothing."

He crushed the wood into his chest, right where his heart used to beat, with enough force to punch through a granite slab. I was totally frozen with panic until he laughed.

"You should see your face, Bree."

He sifted the splinters of broken wood through his fingers; the shattered root fell to the floor in mangled pieces. Diego brushed at his shirt, though

it was too trashed from all the swimming and digging for the attempt to do any good. We'd both
have to steal more clothes the next time we got
a chance.

"Maybe it's different when a human does it."

"Because you felt so magical when you were
human?"

"I don't know, Diego," I said, exasperated. "I
didn't make up all those stories."

He nodded, suddenly more serious. "What if the
stories are exactly that? Made up."

I sighed. "What difference does it make?"

"Not sure. But if we're going to be smart about
why we're here—why Riley brought us to *her*, why
she's making more of us—then we have to understand
as much as we possibly can." He frowned, every trace
of laughter totally gone from his face now.

I just stared back at him. I didn't have any
answers.

His face softened just a little. "This helps a lot,
you know. Talking about it. Helps me focus."

"Me, too," I said. "I don't know why I never
thought about any of this before. It seems so obvious. But working on it together . . . I don't know. I
can stay on track better."

"Exactly." Diego smiled at me. "I'm really glad
you came out tonight."

"Don't get all gooey on me now."

"What? You don't want to be"—he widened his eyes and his voice went up an octave—"BFFs?" He laughed at the goofy expression.

I rolled my eyes, not totally sure if he was making fun of the expression or of me.

"C'mon, Bree. Be my bestest bud forever. Please?" Still teasing, but his wide smile was natural and . . . hopeful. He held out his hand.

This time I went for a real high five, not realizing until he caught my hand and held it that he'd intended anything else.

It was shockingly weird to touch another person after a whole life—because the last three months *were* my whole life—of avoiding any kind of contact. Like touching a sparking downed power line, only to find out that it felt nice.

The smile on my face felt a little lopsided. "Count me in."

"Excellent. Our own private club."

"Very exclusive," I agreed.

He still had my hand. Not shaking it, but not exactly holding it, either. "We need a secret handshake."

"You can be in charge of that one."

"So the super-secret best friends club is called to order, all present, secret handshake to be devised at a later date," he said. "First order of business: Riley. Clueless? Misinformed? Or lying?"

His eyes were on mine as he spoke, wide and sincere. There was no change as he said Riley's name. In that instant, I was sure there was nothing to the stories about Diego and Riley. Diego had just been around more than the others, nothing more. I could trust him.

"Add this to the list," I said. "Agenda. As in, what is his?"

"Bull's-eye. That's exactly what we've got to find out. But first, another experiment."

"That word makes me nervous."

"Trust is an essential part of the whole secret club gig."

He stood up into the extra ceiling space he'd just carved out and started digging again. In a second, his feet were dangling while he held himself up with one hand and excavated with the other.

"You better be digging for garlic," I warned him, and backed up toward the tunnel that led to the sea.

"The stories aren't real, Bree," he called to me. He pulled himself higher into the hole he was making, and the dirt continued to rain down. He was going to fill in his hidey-hole at this rate. Or flood it with light, which would make it even more useless.

I slid most of the way into the escape channel,

just my fingertips and eyes above the edge. The water only came up to my hips. It would take me just the smallest fraction of a second to disappear into the darkness below. I could spend a day not breathing.

I'd never been a fan of fire. This might have been because of some buried childhood memory, or maybe it was more recent. Becoming a vampire was enough fire to last me.

Diego had to be close to the surface. Once again, I struggled with the idea of losing my new and only friend.

"Please stop, Diego," I whispered, knowing he would probably laugh, knowing he wouldn't listen.

"Trust, Bree."

I waited, unmoving.

"Almost . . . ," he muttered. "Okay."

I tensed for the light, or the spark, or the explosion, but Diego dropped back down while it was still dark. In his hand he had a longer root, a thick snaky thing that was almost as tall as me. He gave me an I-told-you-so kind of look.

"I'm not a completely reckless person," he said. He gestured to the root with his free hand. "See— precautions."

With that, he stabbed the root upward into his new hole. There was a final avalanche of pebbles and sand as Diego dropped back onto his knees, getting out of the way. And then a beam of brilliant light— a ray about the thickness of one of Diego's arms— pierced the darkness of the cave. The light made a pillar from the ceiling to the floor, shimmering as the drifting dirt sifted through it. I was icy-still, gripping the ledge, ready to drop.

Diego didn't jerk away or cry out in pain. There was no smell of smoke. The cave was a hundred times lighter than it had been, but it didn't seem to affect him. So maybe his story about shade trees was true. I watched him carefully as he knelt beside the pillar of sunlight, motionless, staring. He seemed fine, but there was a slight change to his skin. A kind of movement, maybe from the settling dust, that reflected the gleam. It looked almost like he was glowing a little.

Maybe it wasn't the dust, maybe it was the burning. Maybe it didn't hurt, and he'd realize it too late. . . .

Seconds passed as we stared at the daylight, motionless.

Then, in a move that seemed both absolutely expected and also completely unthinkable, he held out his hand, palm up, and stretched his arm toward the beam.

I moved faster than I could think, which was

pretty dang fast. Faster than I'd ever moved before.

I tackled Diego into the back wall of the dirt-filled little cave before he could reach that one last inch to put his skin in the light.

The room was filled with a sudden blaze, and I felt the warmth on my leg in the same instant that I realized there wasn't enough room for me to pin Diego to the wall without some part of myself touching the sunlight.

"Bree!" he gasped.

I twisted away from him automatically, rolling myself tight against the wall. It took less than a second, and the whole time I was waiting for the pain to get me. For the flames to hit and then spread like the night I'd met *her*, only faster. The dazzling flash of light was gone. It was just the pillar of sun again.

I looked at Diego's face—his eyes were wide, his mouth hanging open. He was totally still, a sure sign of alarm. I wanted to look down at my leg, but I was afraid to see what was left. This wasn't like Jen ripping my arm off, though that had hurt more. I wasn't going to be able to fix this.

Still no pain yet.

"Bree, did you see *that*?"

I shook my head once quickly. "How bad is it?"

"Bad?"

"My leg," I said through my teeth. "Just tell me what's left."

"Your leg looks fine to me."

I glanced down quickly, and sure enough, there was my foot and my calf, just like before. I wiggled my toes. Fine.

"Does it hurt?" he asked.

I pulled myself off the ground, onto my knees. "Not yet."

"Did you see what happened? The light?"

I shook my head.

"Watch this," he said, kneeling in front of the beam of sunshine again. "And don't shove me out of the way this time. You already proved I'm right." He put his hand out. It was almost as hard to watch this time, even if my leg felt normal.

The second his fingers entered the beam, the cave was filled with a million brilliant rainbow reflections. It was bright as noon in a glass room—light everywhere. I flinched and then shuddered. There was sunlight *all over* me.

"Unreal," Diego whispered. He put the rest of his hand into the beam, and the cave somehow got even brighter. He rolled his hand over to look at the back, then turned it palm up again. The reflections danced like he was spinning a prism.

There was no smell of burning, and he clearly

wasn't in pain. I looked closely at his hand, and it seemed like there were a zillion tiny mirrors in the surface, too small to distinguish separately, all shining back the light with double the intensity of a regular mirror.

"Come here, Bree—you have to try this."

I couldn't think of a reason to refuse, and I *was* curious, but I was also still reluctant as I slid to his side.

"No burn?"

"None. Light doesn't burn us, it just . . . reflects off of us. I guess that's kind of an understatement."

Slow as a human, I reluctantly stretched my fingers into the light. Immediately, reflections blazed away from my skin, making the room so bright that the day outside would look dark in comparison. They weren't exactly reflections, though, because the light was bent and colored, more like crystal. I stuck my whole hand in, and the room got brighter.

"Do you think Riley knows?" I whispered.

"Maybe. Maybe not."

"Why wouldn't he tell us if he did? What would be the point? So we're walking disco balls." I shrugged.

Diego laughed. "I can see where the stories come from. Imagine if you saw this when you were human. Wouldn't you think that the guy over there just burst into flames?"

"If he didn't hang around to chat. Maybe."

"This is incredible," Diego said. With one finger he traced a line across my glowing palm.

Then he jumped to his feet right under the sunbeam, and the room went crazy with light.

"C'mon, let's get out of here." He reached up and pulled himself toward the hole he'd cut to the surface.

You'd think I would have been over it, but I was still nervous to follow. Not wanting to seem like a total chicken, I stayed close on his heels, but I was cringing inside the whole way. Riley had really made his point about burning in the sun; in my mind it was linked to that horrific time of burning as I became a vampire, and I couldn't escape the instinctive panic that filled me every time I thought of it.

Then Diego was out of the hole, and I was next to him half a second later. We stood on a small patch of wild grass, only a few feet from the trees that covered the island. Behind us, it was just a couple of yards to a low bluff, and then the water. Everything around us blazed in the color and light shining off of us.

"Wow," I muttered.

Diego grinned at me, his face beautiful with light, and suddenly, with a deep lurch in my stomach, I realized that the whole BFF thing was way off the mark. For me, anyway. It was just that fast.

His grin softened a little bit into just the hint of a smile. His eyes were wide like mine. All awe and lights. He touched my face, the way he'd touched my hand, as if he was trying to understand the shine.

"So pretty," he said. He left his hand against my cheek.

I'm not sure how long we stood there, smiling like total idiots, blazing away like glass torches. The inlet was empty of boats, which was probably good. No way even a mud-eyed human would have missed us. Not that they could have done anything to us, but I wasn't thirsty, and all the screaming would have ruined the mood.

Eventually a thick cloud drifted in front of the sun. Suddenly we were just us again, though still slightly luminous. Not enough that anyone with eyes duller than a vampire's would notice.

As soon as the shine was gone, my thoughts cleared up and I could think about what was coming next. But even though Diego looked like his normal self again—not made of blazing light, anyway—I knew he would never look the same to me. That tingly sensation in the pit of my stomach was still there. I had the feeling it might be there permanently.

"Do we tell Riley? Do we think he doesn't know?" I asked.

Diego sighed and dropped his hand. "I don't know. Let's think about this while we track them."

"We're going to have to be careful, tracking them in the day. We're kind of noticeable in the sunlight, you know."

He grinned. "Let's be ninjas."

I nodded. "Super-secret ninja club sounds way cooler than the whole BFF thing."

"Definitely better."

It didn't take us more than a few seconds to find the point from which the whole gang had left the island. That was the easy part. Finding where they'd touched ground on the mainland was a whole other problem. We briefly discussed splitting up, then vetoed that idea unanimously. Our logic was really sound—after all, if one of us found something, how would we tell the other?—but mostly I just didn't want to leave him, and I could see he felt the same. Both of us had been without any kind of good companionship our whole lives, and it was just too sweet to waste a minute of it.

There were so many options as to where they could have gone. To the mainland of the peninsula, or to another island, or back to the outskirts of Seattle, or north to Canada. Whenever we pulled down or burned down one of our houses, Riley was always prepared—he always seemed to know exactly where to go next. He must have planned ahead for that stuff, but he didn't let any of us in on the plan.

They could have been anywhere.

Ducking in and out of the water to avoid boats and people really slowed us down. We spent all day with no luck, but neither of us minded. We were having the most fun we'd ever had.

It was such a strange day. Instead of sitting miserably in the darkness trying to tune out the mayhem and swallow my disgust at my hiding place, I was playing ninja with my new best friend, or maybe something more. We laughed a lot while we moved through the patches of shade, throwing rocks at each other like they were Chinese stars.

Then the sun set, and suddenly I was stressed. Would Riley look for us? Would he assume we were fried? Did he know better?

We started moving faster. A lot faster. We'd already circled all the nearby islands, so now we concentrated on the mainland. About an hour after sundown, I caught a familiar scent, and within seconds we were on their trail. Once we found the path of the smell, it was as easy as following a herd of elephants through fresh snow.

We talked about what to do, more serious now as we ran.

"I don't think we should tell Riley," I said. "Let's say we spent all day in your cave before we went looking for them." As I spoke, my paranoia started to grow. "Better yet, let's tell them your cave was filled with water. We couldn't even talk."

"You think Riley's a bad dude, don't you?" he asked quietly after a minute. As he spoke, he took my hand.

"I don't know. But I'd rather act like he was, just in case." I hesitated, then said, "You don't want to think he's bad."

"No," Diego admitted. "He's kind of my friend. I mean, not like you're my friend." He squeezed my fingers. "But more than anyone else. I don't want to think . . ." Diego didn't finish his sentence.

I squeezed his fingers back. "Maybe he's totally decent. Our being careful doesn't change who he is."

"True. Okay, the underwater cave story it is. At least at first . . . I could talk to him about the sun later. I'd rather do it during the day, anyway, when I can prove what I'm claiming right away. And just in case he already knows, but there's some good reason why he told us something else, I should tell him when we're alone. Grab him at dawn, when he's coming back from wherever it is he goes. . . ."

I noticed a ton of *I*'s rather than *we*'s going on in Diego's little speech, and it bothered me. But at the same time, I didn't want much to do with educating Riley. I didn't have the same faith in him Diego did.

"Ninja attack at dawn!" I said to make him laugh. It worked. We started joking again as we tracked our herd of vampires, but I could tell he was thinking serious stuff under the teasing, just like I was.

And I only got more anxious as we ran. Because we were running fast, and there was no way we had the wrong trail, but it was taking too long. We were really getting away from the coast, up and over the closest mountains, off into new territory. This wasn't the normal pattern.

Every house we'd borrowed, whether it was up a mountain or on an island or hidden on a big farm, had a few things in common. The dead owners, the remote locale, and one other thing. They all were sort of focused on Seattle. Oriented around the big city like orbiting moons. Seattle was always the hub, always the target.

We were out of orbit now, and it felt wrong. Maybe it meant nothing, maybe it was just that so many things were changing today. All the truths I'd accepted had been turned upside down and I wasn't in the mood for any other upheavals. Why couldn't Riley have just picked someplace normal?

"Funny they're this far out," Diego murmured, and I could hear the edge in his voice.

"Or scary," I muttered.

He squeezed my hand. "It's cool. The ninja club can handle anything."

"You got a secret handshake yet?"

"Working on it," he promised.

Something started to bug me. It was like I could feel this strange blind spot—I knew there was something I wasn't seeing, but I couldn't put my finger on it. Something obvious . . .

And then, about sixty miles farther west than our usual perimeter, we found the house. It was impossible to mistake the noise. The *boom boom boom* of the bass, the video-game soundtrack, the snarling. Totally our crowd.

I pulled my hand free, and Diego looked at me.

"Hey, I don't even know you," I said in a joking tone. "I haven't had one conversation with you, what with all that water we sat in all day. You could be a ninja or a vampire for all I know."

He grinned. "Same goes for you, stranger." Then low and fast, "Just do the same things you did yesterday. Tomorrow night we'll get out together. Maybe do some reconnaissance, figure out more of what's going on."

"Sounds like a plan. Mum's the word."

He ducked close and *kissed* me—just a peck, but right on the lips. The shock of it zinged through my whole body. Then he said, "Let's do this," and headed down the side of the mountain toward the source of the raucous noise without looking back. Already playing the part.

A little stunned, I followed from a few yards behind, remembering to put the distance between us that I would put between myself and anyone else.

The house was a big, log cabin–style affair, tucked into a hollow in the pines with no sign of any neighbors for miles around. All the windows were black, as if the place were empty, but the whole frame was trembling from the heavy bass in the basement.

Diego went in first, and I tried to move behind him like he was Kevin or Raoul. Hesitant, protecting my space. He found the stairs and charged down with a confident tread.

"Trying to lose me, losers?" he asked.

"Oh, hey, Diego's alive," I heard Kevin answer with a distinct lack of enthusiasm.

"No thanks to you," Diego said as I slipped into the dark basement. The only light came from the various TV screens, but it was way more than any of us needed. I hurried back to where Fred had a whole couch to himself, glad that it was right for me to look anxious because there was no way to hide it. I swallowed hard as the revulsion hit, and curled up in my usual spot on the floor behind the couch. Once I was down, Fred's repellent power seemed to ease up. Or maybe I was just getting used to it.

The basement was more than half empty since it was the middle of the night. All the kids in here had eyes the same as mine—bright, recently fed red.

"Took me a while to clean up your stupid mess," Diego told Kevin. "It was almost dawn by the time I got to what was left of the house. Had to sit in a cave filled with water all day."

"Go tattle to Riley. Whatever."

"I see the little girl made it, too," said a new voice, and I shuddered because it was Raoul. I felt a little bit of relief that he didn't know my name, but mostly I just felt horrified that he'd noticed me at all.

"Yeah, she followed me." I couldn't see Diego, but I knew he was shrugging.

"Aren't you the savior of the hour?" Raoul said snidely.

"We don't get extra points for being morons."

I wished Diego wouldn't taunt Raoul. I hoped Riley would come back soon. Only Riley could curb Raoul even the littlest bit.

But Riley was probably out hunting dregs kids to bring to *her*. Or doing whatever else he did while he was away.

"Interesting attitude you got, Diego. You think that Riley likes you so much he's gonna care if I kill you. I think you're wrong. But either way, for tonight, he already thinks you're dead."

I could hear the others moving. Some probably to back Raoul up, others just getting out of the way. I hesitated in my hiding spot, knowing I wasn't going to let Diego fight them alone, but worried about blowing our cover if it didn't come to that. I hoped Diego had survived this long because he had some crazy combat skills. I wasn't going to have much to offer in that department. There were three members of Raoul's gang here, and some others that might help out just to get on his good side. Would Riley get home before they had time to burn us?

Diego's voice was calm when he answered. "You're really that afraid to take me on alone? Typical."

Raoul snorted. "Does that ever work? I mean, besides in movies. Why should I take you on alone? I don't care about *beating* you. I just want to *end* you."

I rolled into a crouch, tensed to spring.

Raoul kept talking. He liked the sound of his own voice a lot.

"But it's not gonna take all of us to deal with you. These two will take care of the other evidence of your unfortunate survival. Little what's-her-name."

My body felt icy, frozen solid. I tried to shake it off so I could fight my best. Not that it would have made a difference.

And then I felt something else, something totally unexpected—a wave of revulsion so overpowering that I couldn't hold my crouch. I crumpled to the floor, gasping with horror.

I was not the only one to react. I heard disgusted snarls and retching sounds from every corner of the basement. A few people retreated to the edges of the room, where I could see them. They strained against the wall, stretching their necks away as if they could escape the horrible feeling. At least one of these was a member of Raoul's gang.

I heard Raoul's distinctive growl, and then heard it fade as he took off up the stairs. He wasn't the only one to make a break for it. About half of the vampires in the basement cleared out.

I didn't have that choice. I could barely move. And then I realized this had to be because I was so close to Freaky Fred. He was responsible for what was happening. And as horrible as I felt, I was still able to realize that he'd probably just saved my life.

Why?

The sensation of disgust faded slowly. As soon as I could, I crept to the edge of the couch and took in the aftermath. All of Raoul's gang was gone, but

Diego was still there, on the far end of the big room by the TVs. The vampires who remained were slowly relaxing, though everybody looked a little shaken. Most of them were shooting cautious glances in Fred's direction. I peeked at the back of his head, too, though I couldn't see anything. I looked away quickly. Looking at Fred brought back some of the nausea.

"Keep it down."

The deep voice came from Fred. I'd never heard him speak before. Everyone stared and then looked away immediately as the revulsion returned.

So Fred just wanted his peace and quiet. Well, whatever. I was alive because of it. Most likely Raoul would get distracted by some other irritant before dawn and take out his anger on somebody close by. And Riley always came back at the end of the night. He would hear that Diego had been in his cave rather than outside and destroyed by the sun, and Raoul wouldn't have an excuse to attack him or me.

At least, that was the best-case scenario. In the meantime, maybe Diego and I could come up with some plan to steer clear of Raoul.

Again, I had a fleeting sense that I was missing an obvious solution. Before I could figure it out, my thoughts were interrupted.

"Sorry."

The deep, almost silent mutter could only have come from Fred. It looked like I was the only one close enough to really hear. Was he talking to me?

I looked at him again and felt nothing. I couldn't see his face—he had his back to me still. He had thick, wavy blond hair. I'd never noticed that before, not with all the days I'd sat hiding in his shadow. Riley wasn't kidding when he'd said that Fred was special. Gross, but really special. Did Riley have any idea that Fred was so . . . so powerful? He was able to overwhelm a whole room of us in a second.

Though I couldn't see his expression, I had the sense that Fred was waiting for an answer.

"Um, don't apologize," I breathed almost silently. "Thank you."

Fred shrugged.

And then I found I couldn't look at him anymore.

The hours passed slower than usual as I waited for Raoul to come back. From time to time I tried to look at Fred again—to see past the protection he'd created for himself—but I always found myself repelled. If I tried too hard, I ended up gagging.

Thinking about Fred was a good distraction from thinking about Diego. I tried to pretend I didn't care where he was in the room. I didn't look at him but focused on the sound of his breathing—his distinct rhythm—to keep tabs. He sat on the other side of the room from me, listening to his CDs on a laptop. Or maybe pretending to listen, the way I was pretending to read the books from the damp backpack on my shoulders. I flipped pages at my usual rate, but I didn't take anything in. I was waiting for Raoul.

Luckily, Riley came first. Raoul and his cohorts were right behind him, but not as loud and obnoxious as usual. Maybe Fred had taught them a little respect.

Probably not, though. More likely Fred had just angered them. I really hoped Fred never let his guard slip.

Riley went to Diego right away; I listened with my back to them, eyes on my book. In my peripheral vision, I saw some of Raoul's idiots wandering, looking for their favorite games or whatever they'd been doing before Fred had driven them out. Kevin was one of them, but he seemed to be looking for something more specific than entertainment. Several times his eyes tried to focus on where I was sitting, but Fred's aura kept him at bay. He gave up after a few minutes, looking a little sick.

"I heard you made it back," Riley said, sounding genuinely pleased. "I can always count on you, Diego."

"No problem," Diego said in a relaxed voice.

"Unless you count holding my breath all day as a negative."

Riley laughed. "Don't cut it so close next time. Set a better example for the babies."

Diego just laughed with him. From the corner of my eye, it seemed like Kevin relaxed some. Was he really that worried about Diego getting him in trouble? Maybe Riley listened to Diego more than I realized. I wondered whether that was why Raoul had gotten crazy before.

Was it a good thing if Diego was that in with Riley after all? Maybe Riley was okay. That relationship didn't compromise what we had, did it?

Time didn't pass any faster after the sun was up. It was crowded and unstable in the basement, like every day. If vampires could get hoarse, Riley would have lost his voice entirely from the yelling. A couple of kids temporarily lost limbs, but nobody got torched. The music warred with the game tracks, and I was glad I didn't get headaches. I tried reading my books, but I ended up just flipping through one after the other, not caring enough to make my eyes focus on the words. I left them in a neat stack by the end of the couch for Fred. I always left my books for him, though I never could tell whether he read them. Couldn't look at him closely enough to see what, exactly, he did with his time.

At least Raoul never looked my way. Neither did Kevin or any of the others. My hiding place was as effective as ever. I couldn't see if Diego was smart enough to ignore me, because I was ignoring him so thoroughly. No one could suspect that we were a team, except maybe Fred. Had Fred been paying attention as I prepared to fight alongside Diego? Even if he had, I didn't worry too much about it. If Fred felt any particular ill will toward me, he could have let me die last night. Would have been easy.

It got louder as the sun started to go down. We couldn't see the light fading here underground, with all of the windows upstairs covered just in case. But waiting through so many long days gave you a good sense for when one was almost over. Kids started getting antsy, bugging Riley about whether they could go out.

"Kristie, you were out last night," Riley said, and you could hear the patience wearing thin in his voice. "Heather, Jim, Logan—go ahead. Warren, your eyes are dark, go along with them. Hey, Sara, I'm not blind—get back here."

The kids he shut down sulked in the corners, some of them waiting for Riley to leave so they could sneak out in spite of his rules.

"Um, Fred, must be about your turn," Riley said,

not looking in our direction. I heard Fred sigh as he got to his feet. Everyone cringed as he moved through the center of the room, even Riley. But unlike the others, Riley smiled a little to himself. He liked his vampire with skills.

I felt naked with Fred gone. Anyone could focus on me now. I held perfectly still, head down, doing everything in my power not to call attention to myself.

Lucky for me, Riley was in a hurry tonight. He barely paused to glare at the people who were clearly edging for the door, let alone threaten them, as he headed out himself. Normally he'd give us some variant on the usual speech about keeping a low profile, but not tonight. He seemed preoccupied, anxious. I'd have bet he was going to see *her*. That made me less excited about catching up with him at dawn.

I waited for Kristie and three of her usual companions to head out, and I slipped out in their wake, trying to look like part of the entourage without irritating them. I didn't look at Raoul, I didn't look at Diego. I concentrated on seeming inconsequential— no one to notice. Just some random vampire chick.

Once we were out of the house, I split off from Kristie immediately and beat it into the woods. I hoped only Diego would care enough to follow my scent. Halfway up the side of the nearest mountain, I made my perch in the top branches of a big spruce that cleared its neighbors by several meters. I had a pretty good view of anyone who might try to track me.

Turns out I was being overcautious. Maybe I'd been too cautious all day. Diego was the only one to come looking. I saw him from a distance and back-tracked to meet him.

"Long day," he said, giving me a hug. "Your plan is hard."

I hugged him back, marveling at how comfortable this was. "Maybe I'm just being paranoid."

"Sorry about Raoul. That was close."

I nodded. "Good thing Fred is so disgusting."

"I wonder if Riley knows how potent that kid is."

"Doubt it. I've never seen him do *that* before, and I spend a lot of time around him."

"Well, that's Freaky Fred's business. We have our own secret to tell Riley."

I shuddered. "Still not sure that's a good idea."

"We won't know until we see how Riley reacts."

"I don't really like not knowing, as a general rule."

Diego's eyes narrowed speculatively. "How do you feel about adventure?"

"Depends."

"Well, I was thinking about club priorities. You know, about finding out as much as we can."

"And . . . ?"

"I think we should follow Riley. Find out what he's doing."

I stared. "But he'll know we tracked him. He'll catch our scents."

"I know. This is how I figure it. I follow his scent. You keep clear by a few hundred yards and follow my sound. Then Riley only knows I followed him, and I can tell him it's because I had something important to share. That's when I do the big reveal with the disco ball effect. And I'll see what he says." His eyes narrowed as he examined me. "But you . . . you just play it close to the chest for now, okay? I'll tell you if he's cool about it."

"What if he comes back early from wherever he's going? Don't you want it to be close to dawn so you can glitter?"

"Yes . . . that's definitely a possible problem. And it might affect the way the conversation goes. But I think we should risk it. He seemed like he was in a hurry tonight, didn't he? Like maybe he needs all night for whatever he's doing?"

"Maybe. Or maybe he was just in a big hurry to see *her*. You know, we might not want to surprise him if she's nearby." We both winced.

"True. Still . . ." He frowned. "Doesn't it feel like whatever's coming is getting close? Like we might not have forever to figure this out?"

I nodded unhappily. "Yeah, it does."

"So let's take our chances. Riley trusts me, and I have a good reason for wanting to talk to him."

I thought about this strategy. Though I'd only known him for a day, really, I was still aware that this level of paranoia was out of character for Diego.

"This elaborate plan of yours . . . ," I said.

"What about it?" he asked.

"It sounds kind of like a solo plan. Not so much a club adventure. At least, not when it comes to the dangerous part."

He made a face that told me I'd caught him.

"This is my idea. I'm the one who . . ." He hesitated, having trouble with the next word. ". . . trusts Riley. I'm the only one who's going to risk getting on his bad side if I'm wrong."

Chicken as I was, this didn't fly with me. "Clubs don't work that way."

He nodded, his expression unclear. "Okay, we'll think about it as we go."

I didn't think he really meant it.

"Stay in the trees, track me from above, 'kay?" he said.

"Okay."

He headed back toward the log cabin, moving fast. I followed through the branches, most of them so close-packed that I only rarely had to really leap from one tree to another. I kept my movements as small as possible, hoping that the bending of the boughs under my weight would just look like wind. It was a breezy night, which would help. It was cold for summer, not that the temperature bothered me.

Diego caught Riley's scent outside the house without trouble and then loped after it quickly while I trailed several yards back and about a hundred yards north, higher on the slope than he was. When the trees were really thick, he'd rustle a trunk now and again so I wouldn't lose him.

We kept on, with him running and me impersonating a flying squirrel, for only fifteen minutes or so before I saw Diego slow down. We must have been getting close. I moved higher in the branches, looking for a tree with a good view. I scaled one that towered over its neighbors, and scanned the scene.

Less than half a mile away was a large gap in the trees, an open field that covered several acres. Near the center of the space, closer to the trees on its east side, was what looked like an oversized gingerbread house. Painted bright pink, green, and white, it was elaborate to the point of ridiculousness, with fancy trim and finials on every conceivable edge. It was the kind of thing I would have laughed at in a more relaxed situation.

Riley was nowhere in sight, but Diego had come to a complete stop below, so I assumed this was the end point of our pursuit. Maybe this was the replacement house Riley was preparing for when the big log cabin crumbled. Except that it was smaller than any of the other houses we'd stayed in, and it didn't look like it had a basement. And it was even farther away from Seattle than the last one.

Diego looked up at me, and I signaled for him to join me. He nodded and retraced his trail a little ways. Then he made an enormous leap—I wondered if I could have jumped that high, even as young and strong as I was—and caught a branch about halfway up the closest tree. Unless someone was being extraordinarily vigilant, no one ever would have noticed that Diego'd made a side trip off his path. Even still, he jumped around in the treetops, making sure his trail did not lead directly to mine.

When he finally decided it was safe to join me, he took my hand right away. Silently, I nodded toward the gingerbread house. One corner of his mouth twitched.

Simultaneously we started edging toward the east side of the house, keeping high up in the trees. We got as close as we dared—leaving a few trees as cover between the house and ourselves—and then sat silently, listening.

The breeze turned helpfully gentle, and we could hear something. Strange little brushing, ticking sounds. At first I didn't recognize what I was hearing, but then Diego twitched another little smile, puckered his lips, and silently kissed the air in my direction.

Kissing didn't sound the same with vampires as it did with humans. No soft, fleshy, liquid-filled cells to squish against each other. Just stone lips, no give. I had heard one kiss between vampires before—Diego's touch to my lips last night—but I never would have made the connection. It was so far from what I'd expected to find here.

This knowledge spun everything around in my head. I had assumed Riley was going to see *her*, whether to receive instructions or bring her new recruits, I didn't know. But I had never imagined stumbling across some kind of . . . love nest. How could Riley kiss *her*? I shuddered and glanced at Diego. He looked faintly horrified, too, but he shrugged.

I thought back to that last night of humanity, flinching as I remembered the vivid burning. I tried to recall the moments just before that, through all the fuzziness. . . . First there was the creeping fear that had built as Riley pulled up to the dark house, the feeling of safety I'd had in the bright burger joint dissolving entirely. I was holding back, edging away, and then he'd grabbed my arm with a steel grip and yanked me out of the car like I was a doll, weightless. Terror and disbelief as he'd leaped the ten yards to the door. Terror and then pain leaving no room for disbelief as he broke my arm dragging me through the door into the black house. And then the voice.

As I focused on the memory, I could hear it again. High and singsong, like a little girl's, but grouchy. A child throwing a tantrum.

I remembered what she'd said. "Why did you even bring this one? It's too small." Something close to that, I thought. The words might not be exactly right, but that was the meaning.

I was sure Riley had sounded eager to please when he answered, afraid of disappointing. "But she's another body. Another distraction, at least."

I think I'd whimpered then, and he'd shaken me painfully, but he hadn't spoken to me again. It was like I was a dog, not a person.

"This whole night has been a waste," the child's voice had complained. "I've killed them all. Ugh!"

I remembered that the house had shuddered then, as if a car had collided with the frame. I realized now that she'd probably just kicked something in frustration.

"Fine. I guess even a little one is better than nothing, if this is the best you can do. And I'm so full now I should be able to stop."

Riley's hard fingers had disappeared then and left me alone with the voice. I'd been too panicked at that point to make a sound. I'd just closed my eyes, though I was already totally blind in the darkness. I didn't scream until something cut into my neck, burning like a blade coated in acid.

I cringed back from the memory, trying to push the next part from my mind. Instead I concentrated on that short conversation. She hadn't sounded like she was talking to her lover or even her friend. More like she was talking to an employee. One she didn't like much and might fire soon.

But the strange vampire kissing sounds continued. Someone sighed in contentment.

I frowned at Diego. This exchange didn't tell us much. How long did we need to stay?

He just held his head on the side, listening carefully.

And after a few more minutes of patience, the low, romantic sounds were suddenly interrupted.

"How many?"

The voice was muted by distance, but still distinct. And recognizable. High, almost a trill. Like a spoiled young girl.

"Twenty-two," Riley answered, sounding proud. Diego and I exchanged a sharp glance. There were twenty-two of us, at last count, anyway. They must be talking about us.

"I thought I'd lost two more to the sun, but one of my older kids is . . . obedient," Riley continued. There was almost an affectionate sound to his voice when he spoke of Diego as one of his *kids*. "He has an underground place—he hid himself with the younger one."

"Are you sure?"

There was a long pause, this time with no sounds of romance. Even from this distance, I thought I could feel some tension.

"Yeah. He's a good kid, I'm sure."

Another strained pause. I didn't understand her question. What did she mean, *are you sure*? Did she think he'd heard the story from someone else rather than seeing Diego for himself?

"Twenty-two is good," she mused, and the tension seemed to dissolve. "How is their behavior developing? Some of them are almost a year old. Do they still follow the normal patterns?"

"Yes," Riley said. "Everything you told me to do worked flawlessly. They don't think—they just do what they've always done. I can always distract them with thirst. It keeps them under control."

I frowned at Diego. Riley didn't want us to think. Why?

"You've done so well," our creator cooed, and there was another kiss. "Twenty-two!"

"Is it time?" Riley asked eagerly.

Her answer came back fast, like a slap. "No! I haven't decided when."

"I don't understand."

"You don't need to. It's enough for you to know that our enemies have great powers. We cannot be too careful." Her voice softened, turned sugary again. "But all twenty-two still alive. Even with what *they* are capable of . . . what good will it be against twenty-two?" She let out a tinkling little laugh.

Diego and I had not looked away from each other throughout all this, and I could see in his eyes now that his thoughts were the same as mine. Yes, we'd been created for a purpose, as we'd guessed. We had an enemy. Or, our creator had an enemy. Did the distinction matter?

"Decisions, decisions," she muttered. "Not yet. Maybe one more handful, just to be sure."

"Adding more might actually decrease our numbers," Riley cautioned hesitantly, as if being careful not to upset her. "It's always unstable when a new group is introduced."

"True," she agreed, and I imagined Riley sighing in relief that she was not upset.

Abruptly Diego looked away from me, staring out across the meadow. I hadn't heard any movement from the house, but maybe she had come out. My head whipped around at the same time the rest of me turned to a statue, and I saw what had startled Diego.

Four figures were crossing the open field to the house. They had entered the clearing from the west, the point farthest from where we hid. They all wore long, dark cloaks with deep hoods, so at first I thought they were people. Weird people, but just humans all the same, because none of the vampires I knew had matching Goth clothes. And none moved in a way that was so smooth and controlled and . . . elegant. But then I realized that none of the humans I'd ever seen could move that way, either, and what's more, they couldn't do it so quietly. The dark-cloaks skimmed across the long grass in absolute silence. So either these were vampires, or they were something else supernatural. Ghosts, maybe. But if they were vampires, they were vampires I didn't know, and that meant they might very well be these enemies she was talking about. If so, we should get the hell out of Dodge right *now*, because we didn't have twenty other vampires on our side at the moment.

I almost took off then, but I was too afraid to draw the attention of the cloaked figures.

So I watched them move smoothly forward, noticing other things about them. How they stayed in a perfect diamond formation that never was the slightest bit out of line no matter how the terrain changed under their feet. How the one at the point of the diamond was much smaller than the others, and its cloak was darker, too. How they didn't seem to be tracking their way in—not trying to follow the path of any scent. They simply knew their way. Maybe they were invited.

They moved directly toward the house, and I felt like it might be safe to breathe again when they started silently up the steps toward the front door. They weren't coming straight for Diego and me, at least. When they were out of sight, we could disappear into the sound of the next breeze through the trees, and they would never know we'd been here.

I looked at Diego and twitched my head slightly toward the way we'd come. He narrowed his eyes and held up one finger. Oh great, he wanted to stay. I rolled my eyes at him, though I was so afraid, I was surprised I was capable of sarcasm.

We both looked back to the house. The cloaked things had let themselves in silently, but I realized that neither she nor Riley had spoken since we'd caught sight of the visitors. They must have heard something or known in some other way that they were in danger.

"Don't bother," a very clear, monotone voice commanded lazily. It was not as high-pitched as our creator's, but it still sounded girlish to me. "I think you know who we are, so you must know that there is no point in trying to surprise us. Or hide from us. Or fight us. Or run."

A deep, masculine chuckle that did not belong to Riley echoed menacingly through the house.

"Relax," instructed the first inflectionless voice— the cloaked girl. Her voice had that distinctive ring that made me certain she was a vampire, not a ghost or any other kind of nightmare. "We're not here to destroy you. Yet."

There was a moment of silence, and then some barely audible movements. A shifting of positions.

"If you are not here to kill us, then . . . what?" our creator asked, strained and shrill.

"We seek to know your intentions here. Specifically, if they involve . . . a certain local clan," the cloaked girl explained. "We wonder if they have anything to do with the mayhem you've created here. *Illegally* created."

Diego and I frowned simultaneously. None of this made sense, but the last part was the weirdest.

What could be illegal for vampires? What cop, what judge, what prison could have power over us?

"Yes," our creator hissed. "My plans are *all* about them. But we can't move yet. It's tricky." A petulant note crept into her voice at the end.

"Trust me, we know the difficulties better than you. It is remarkable that you've managed to keep off the radar, so to speak, for this long. Tell me"—a hint of interest colored the monotone—"how are you doing it?"

Our creator hesitated, and then spoke all in a rush. Almost as if there had been some silent intimidation. "I haven't made the decision," she spit out. Then she added more slowly, unwillingly, "To attack. I've never decided to *do* anything with them."

"Rough, but effective," the cloaked girl said. "Unfortunately, your period of deliberation has come to a close. You must decide—*now*—what you will do with your little army." Both Diego's and my eyes widened at that word. "Otherwise, it will be our duty to punish you as the law demands. This reprieve, however short, troubles me. It is not our way. I suggest you give us what assurances you can . . . quickly."

"We'll go at once!" Riley volunteered anxiously, and there was a sharp hiss.

"We'll go as soon as possible," our creator amended furiously. "There is much to do. I assume you wish us to succeed? Then I must have a little time to get them trained—instructed—fed!"

There was a short pause.

"Five days. We will come for you then. And there is no rock you can hide under or speed at which you can flee that will save you. If you have not made your attack by the time we come, you will burn." This was said with no menace other than an absolute certainty.

"And if I *have* made my attack?" our creator asked, shaken.

"We'll see," the cloaked girl answered in a brighter tone than she'd used yet. "I suppose that all depends on how successful you are. Work hard to please us." The last command was given in a flat, hard pitch that made me feel a strange chill in the center of my body.

"Yes," our creator snarled.

"Yes," Riley echoed in a whisper.

A second later the cloaked vampires were noiselessly exiting the house. Neither Diego nor I so much as took a breath for five minutes after they'd disappeared. Inside the house, our creator and Riley were just as quiet. Another ten minutes passed in total stillness.

I touched Diego's arm. This was our chance to get out of here. At the moment, I wasn't so afraid of Riley anymore. I wanted to get as far away as I could from those dark-cloaks. I wanted the safety of numbers waiting back in the log cabin, and I figured that was exactly how our creator felt, too. Why she'd made so many of us in the first place. There were some things out there scarier than I'd imagined.

Diego hesitated, still listening, and a second later his patience was rewarded.

"Well," she whispered inside the house, "now they know."

Was she talking about the cloaks or the mysterious clan? Which one was the enemy she'd mentioned before the drama?

"That doesn't matter. We outnumber—"

"Any warning *matters*!" she growled, cutting him off. "There is so much to do. Only five days!" She groaned. "No more messing around. You start tonight."

"I won't fail you!" Riley promised.

Crap. Diego and I moved at the same time, leaping from our perch into the next tree over, flying back the way we'd come. Riley was in a hurry now, and if he found Diego's trail after all that had just passed with the cloaks, and no Diego there at the end of it . . .

"I've got to get back and be waiting," Diego whispered to me as we raced. "Lucky it's not in view of the house! Don't want him to know I heard."

"We should talk to him together."

"Too late for that. He'd notice that your scent wasn't on the trail. Looks suspicious."

"Diego . . ." He'd trapped me into sitting this one out.

We were back to the spot where he'd joined me. He spoke in a rushed whisper.

"Stick to the plan, Bree. I'll tell him what I planned to tell him. It's not close to dawn, but that's just how it has to be. If he doesn't believe me . . ." Diego shrugged. "He's got bigger things to worry about than me having an overactive imagination. Maybe he'll be more likely to listen now—looks like we need all the help we can get, and being able to move around in the day can't hurt."

"Diego . . . ," I repeated, not knowing what else to say.

He looked into my eyes, and I waited for his lips to twitch into that easy smile, for him to make some joke about ninjas or BFFs.

He didn't. Instead, he leaned in slowly, never moving his eyes from mine, and kissed me. His smooth lips pressed against mine for one long second while we stared at each other.

Then he leaned away and sighed. "Get home, hide

behind Fred, and act clueless. I'll be right behind you."

"Be careful."

I grabbed his hand and squeezed it hard, then let go. Riley had spoken of Diego affectionately. I would have to hope that affection was real. There wasn't another choice.

Diego disappeared into the trees, quiet as a rustling breeze. I didn't waste time looking after him. I sprinted through the branches in a direct line back to the house. I hoped my eyes were still bright enough from last night's meal to explain my absence. Just a quick hunt. Got lucky—found a lone hiker. Nothing out of the ordinary.

The sound of the thudding music that greeted my approach was accompanied by the unmistakable sweet, smoky scent of a burning vampire. My panic went into overdrive. I could just as easily die inside the house as outside. But there was no other way. I didn't slow, just rushed down the stairs straight to the corner where I could barely make out Freaky Fred standing. Looking for something to do? Tired of sitting? I had no idea what he was up to, and I didn't care. I would stick tight to him until Riley and Diego got back.

In the middle of the floor was a smoldering heap that was too big to be just a leg or an arm. So much for Riley's twenty-two.

No one seemed terribly concerned about the smoking remains. The sight was too common.

As I hurried closer to Fred, for once the sense of disgust didn't get stronger. Instead, it faded. He didn't seem to notice me, just went on reading the book he held. One of those I'd left him a few days ago. I had no problem seeing what he was doing now that I was close to where he was leaning against the back of the couch. I hesitated, wondering why that was. Could he turn his nausea thing off when he wanted? Did that mean we both were unprotected right now? At least Raoul wasn't home yet, thankfully, though Kevin was.

For the first time ever, I really saw what Fred looked like. He was tall, maybe six two, with the thick, curly blond hair I'd noticed once before. He was broad-shouldered and muscular. He looked older than most of the others—like a college student, not a high school kid. And—this was the part that surprised me most for some reason—he was good-looking. As handsome as anyone else, maybe even handsomer than most. I didn't know why that was so trippy for me. I guessed just because I always associated him with revulsion.

I felt weird for staring. I glanced quickly around the room to see if anyone had noticed that Fred was normal—and pretty—for the moment. No one was looking our way. I stole a fast peek at Kevin, ready to shift my focus at once if he noticed, but his eyes were concentrated on some point to the left of where we stood. He was frowning slightly. Before I could look away, his gaze skipped right over to me and settled on my right side. His frown deepened. Like . . . he was trying to see me and couldn't.

I felt the corners of my mouth twitch into not quite a grin. There was too much to worry about to really enjoy Kevin's blindness. I looked back at Fred, wondering if the gross-out factor would return, only to see that he was smiling with me. Smiling, he was really spectacular.

Then the moment was over, and Fred went back to his book. I didn't move for a while, waiting for something to happen. For Diego to come through the door. Or Riley with Diego. Or Raoul. Or for the nausea to hit again, or for Kevin to glare in my direction, or for the next fight to break out. Something.

When nothing did, I eventually pulled myself together and did what I should have been doing— pretending nothing unusual was going on. I grabbed a book from the pile near Fred's feet and then sat down right there and acted like I was reading. It was probably one of the same books I'd pretended to read yesterday, but it didn't look familiar. I flipped through the pages, again taking nothing in.

My mind was racing around in tight little circles. Where was Diego? How had Riley reacted to his story? What had it all meant—the talk before the cloaks, the talk after the cloaks?

I worked through it, going backward, trying to assemble the pieces into a recognizable picture. The vampire world had some kind of police, and they were damn scary. This wild group of months-old vampires was supposed to be an army, and this army was somehow illegal. Our creator had an enemy. Strike that, two enemies. We were going to attack one of them in five days, or else the other ones, the scary cloaks, were going to attack her—or us, or both. We would be trained for this attack . . . as soon as Riley got back. I snuck a glance at the door, then forced my eyes back to the page in front of me. And then the stuff before the visitors. She was worrying about some decision. She was pleased that she had so many vampires—so many *soldiers*. Riley was happy that Diego and I had survived. . . . He'd said he thought he'd lost two more to the sun, so that must mean he didn't know how vampires *really* reacted to sunlight. What she'd said was strange, though. She'd asked if he was *sure*. Sure Diego had survived? Or . . . sure that Diego's story was true?

The last thought frightened me. Did she already

know that the sun didn't hurt us? If she did know, then why had she lied to Riley and, through him, to us?

Why would she want to keep us in the dark—literally? Was it very important to her that we stay ignorant? Important enough to get Diego in trouble? I was working myself into a real panic, frozen solid. If I still could sweat, I would have been sweating now. I had to refocus to turn the next page, to keep my eyes down.

Was Riley deceived, or was he in on it, too? When Riley'd said he thought he'd lost two more to the sun, did he mean the sun literally . . . or the lie about the sun?

If it was the second option, then to know the truth meant being *lost*. Panic scattered my thoughts.

I tried to be rational and make sense of it. It was harder without Diego. Having someone to talk to, to interact with, sharpened my ability to concentrate. Without that, fear sucked at the edges of my thoughts, twisted with the always-present thirst. The lure of blood was constantly close to the surface. Even now, decently well fed, I could feel the burn and the need.

Think about her, *think about Riley*, I told myself. I had to understand why they would lie—if they were lying—so that I could try to figure out what it would mean to them that Diego knew their secret.

If they hadn't lied, if they'd just told us all that the day was as safe for us as the night, how would that change things? I imagined what it would be like if we didn't have to be contained in a blacked-out basement all day, if the twenty-one of us—maybe fewer now, depending on how the hunting parties were getting along—were free to do what we wanted whenever we wanted to.

We would want to hunt. That was a given.

If we didn't have to come back, if we didn't have to hide . . . well, many of us wouldn't come back very regularly. It was hard to focus on the return while the thirst was in charge. But Riley had drilled so deeply into all of us the threat of burning, of a return of that hideous pain we'd all experienced once. That was the reason we could stop ourselves. Self-preservation, the only instinct stronger than thirst.

So the threat kept us together. There were other hiding places, like Diego's cave, but who else thought about that kind of thing? We had a place to go, a base, so we went to it. Clear heads were not a vampire specialty. Or, at least, they weren't the specialty of *young* vampires. Riley was clearheaded. Diego was more clearheaded than I was. Those cloaked vampires were terrifyingly focused. I shuddered. So the routine wouldn't control us forever. What would they do when we were older, clearer? It struck me that nobody was older than Riley. Everyone here was new. She needed a bunch of us now for this mystery enemy. But what about afterward?

I had a strong feeling that I didn't want to be around for that part. And I suddenly realized something stupendously obvious. It was the solution that had tickled the edges of my understanding before, when I was tracking the vampire herd to this place with Diego.

I didn't have to be around for that part. I didn't have to be around for one more night.

I was a statue again as I thought over this stunning idea.

If Diego and I hadn't known where the gang was most likely headed, would we ever have found them? Probably not. And that was a big group leaving a wide trail. What if it were a single vampire, one who could leap up onto the land, maybe into a tree, without leaving a trail at the edge of the water. . . . Just one, or maybe two vampires who could swim as far out to sea as they wanted . . . Who could return to land anywhere . . . Canada, California, Chile, China . . .

You would never be able to find those two vampires. They would be gone. Disappeared like they'd gone up in smoke.

We didn't have to come back the other night! We *shouldn't* have! Why hadn't I thought of it then?

But . . . would Diego have agreed? I was abruptly not so sure of myself. Was Diego more loyal to Riley after all? Would he have felt it was his responsibility to stand by Riley? He'd known Riley a lot longer— he'd really only known me a day. Was he closer to Riley than he was to me?

I pondered that, frowning.

Well, I would find out as soon as we had a minute alone. And then maybe, if our secret club really meant something, it wouldn't matter what our creator had planned for us. We could disappear, and Riley would have to make do with nineteen vampires, or make some new ones quick. Either way, not our problem.

I couldn't wait to tell Diego my plan. My gut instinct was that he would feel the same. Hopefully.

Suddenly, I wondered if this was what had really happened to Shelly and Steve and the other kids who had disappeared. I knew they hadn't burned in the sun. Had Riley only claimed he'd seen their ashes as another way to keep the rest of us afraid and dependent on him? Returning home to him every dawn? Maybe Shelly and Steve had just set off on their own. No more Raoul. No enemies or armies threatening their immediate future.

Maybe that's what Riley had meant by *lost to the sun*. Runaways. In which case, he'd be happy that Diego hadn't bailed, right?

If only Diego and I *had* taken off! We could be free, too, like Shelly and Steve. No rules, no fear of the sunrise.

Again, I imagined the whole horde of us on the loose without a curfew. I could see Diego and me moving like ninjas through the shade. But I could also see Raoul, Kevin, and the rest, sparkling disco-ball monsters in the center of a busy downtown street, the bodies piling up, the screaming, the helicopters whirring, the soft, helpless cops with their dinky little bullets that wouldn't make a dent, the cameras, the panic that would spread so fast as the pictures bounced swiftly around the globe.

Vampires wouldn't be a secret for very long. Even Raoul couldn't kill people fast enough to keep the story from spreading.

There was a chain of logic here, and I tried to grasp it before I could be distracted again.

One, humans didn't know about vampires. Two, Riley encouraged us to be inconspicuous, not to attract the notice of humans and educate them otherwise. Three, Diego and I had decided that all vampires must be following that guideline, or else the world would know about us. Four, they must have a reason for doing so, and it wasn't the little popguns of the human police that motivated them. Yeah, the reason must be pretty important to make all vampires hide all day long in stuffy basements. Maybe reason enough to make Riley and our creator lie to us, terrify us about the burning sun. Maybe it was a reason Riley would explain to Diego, and since it was so important and he was so responsible, Diego would promise to keep the secret and they would be cool with that. Sure they would. But what if what actually happened to Shelly and Steve was that they'd discovered the shiny skin thing and *not* run? What if they'd gone to Riley?

And, crap, there went the next step in my logical path. The chain dissolved and I started panicking about Diego again.

As I stressed, I realized that I'd been thinking things through for a while. I could feel dawn coming on. No more than an hour away. So where was Diego? Where was Riley?

As I thought this, the door opened and Raoul leaped down the stairs, laughing with his buddies. I hunched down, leaning closer to Fred. Raoul didn't notice us. He looked at the crispy-fried vampire in the center of the floor and laughed harder. His eyes were brilliant red.

On the nights Raoul went hunting, he never

came home till he had to. He would keep feeding as long as he could. So dawn must have been even closer than I'd thought.

Riley must have demanded that Diego prove his words. That was the only explanation. And they were waiting for the dawn. Only . . . that would mean that Riley *didn't* know the truth, that our creator was lying to him, too. Or did it? My thoughts twisted up again.

Kristie showed up minutes later with three of her gang. She reacted indifferently to the pile of ashes. I did a quick head count as two more hunters hurried through the door. Twenty vampires. Everyone was home except Diego and Riley. The sun would rise at any moment.

The door at the top of the basement stairs creaked as someone opened it. I sprang to my feet.

Riley entered. He shut the door behind him. He walked down the stairs.

No one followed.

Before I could process this, Riley roared out an animalistic shriek of rage. He was staring down at the ashy remains on the floor, his eyes bulging in fury. Everyone stood silent, immobile. We'd all seen Riley lose his temper, but this was something different.

Riley spun and raked his fingers through a blaring

speaker, then ripped it from the wall and hurled it across the room. Jen and Kristie dodged out of the way as it exploded into the far wall, sending up a cloud of pulverized drywall dust. Riley smashed the sound system with his foot, and the thudding bass went silent. Then he leaped to where Raoul stood, and grabbed him by the throat.

"I wasn't even here!" Raoul yelled, looking afraid—I'd never seen *that* before.

Riley growled hideously and threw Raoul as he'd thrown the speaker. Jen and Kristie jumped out of the way again. Raoul's body crashed right through the wall, leaving an enormous hole.

Riley caught Kevin by the shoulder and—with a familiar screech—ripped off his right hand. Kevin cried out in pain and tried to twist out of Riley's grip. Riley kicked him in the side. Another harsh shriek and Riley had the rest of Kevin's arm. He tore the arm in half at the elbow and threw the pieces hard into Kevin's anguished face—*smack, smack, smack*, like a hammer striking stone.

"What is *wrong* with you?" Riley screamed at us. "Why are you all *so stupid*?" He made a grab for the blond Spider-Man kid, but that kid leaped out of his way. His jump left him too close to Fred, and he stumbled back toward Riley again, gagging.

"Do *any* of you have a brain?"

Riley smacked a kid named Dean into the entertainment center, shattering it, then caught another
girl—Sara—and tore her left ear and a handful of
hair from her head. She snarled in anguish.

It became suddenly obvious that Riley was doing
a very dangerous thing. There were a lot of us in
here. Already Raoul was back, with Kristie and
Jen—usually his enemies—flanking him defen-
sively. A few others banded together in clusters
around the room.

I wasn't sure if Riley was aware of the threat or
if his rant came to an end naturally. He took a deep
breath. He tossed Sara her ear and the hair. She
recoiled away from him, licking the torn edge of her
ear, coating it with venom so that it would reattach.
There was no remedy for the hair, though; Sara was
going to have a bald spot.

"Listen to me!" Riley said, quiet but fierce. "All
our lives depend on you listening to what I'm saying now and *thinking*! We are all going to *die*. Every
one of us, you and me, too, if you can't act like you
have brains for just a few short days!"

This was nothing like his usual lectures and
pleadings for control. He definitely had everyone's
attention.

"It's time for you to grow up and take responsibility for yourselves. Do you think you get to live

like this for *free*? That all the blood in Seattle doesn't have a *price*?"

The little clusters of vampires no longer seemed threatening. Everyone was wide-eyed, some exchanging mystified glances. I saw Fred's head turn toward me in my peripheral vision, but I didn't meet his gaze. My attention was focused on two things: Riley, just in case he started to attack again, and the door. The door that was still closed.

"Are you listening now? Really listening?" Riley paused, but no one nodded. The room was very still. "Let me explain to you the precarious situation we are all in. I'll try to keep it simple for the slowest ones. Raoul, Kristie, come here."

He motioned to the leaders of the two largest gangs, allied for this brief moment against him. Neither of them moved toward him. They braced themselves, Kristie baring her teeth.

I expected Riley to soften, to apologize. To placate them and then persuade them to do what he wanted. But this was a different Riley.

"Fine," he snapped. "We're going to need leaders if we're going to survive, but apparently neither of you is up to the task. I thought you had aptitude. I was wrong. Kevin, Jen, please join me as the heads of this team."

Kevin looked up in surprise. He had just finished

putting his arm back together. Though his expression was wary, it was also unmistakably flattered. He slowly got to his feet. Jen looked at Kristie as if waiting for permission. Raoul ground his teeth together.

The door at the top of the stairs did not open.

"Are you not able, either?" Riley asked, irritated.

Kevin took a step toward Riley, but then Raoul rushed him, leaping across the long room in two low bounds. He shoved Kevin against the wall without a word and then stood by Riley's right shoulder.

Riley permitted himself a tiny smile. The manipulation wasn't subtle, but it was effective.

"Kristie or Jen, who will lead us?" Riley asked with a hint of amusement in his voice.

Jen was still waiting for a sign from Kristie as to what she should do. Kristie glowered at Jen for an instant, then flipped her sandy hair out of her face and darted to stand on Riley's other side.

"That took too long to decide," Riley said seriously. "We don't have the luxury of time. We don't get to fool around anymore. I've let you all do pretty much whatever you feel like, but that ends tonight."

He looked around the room, meeting everyone's eyes, making sure we were listening. I held his gaze for only a second when it was my turn, and then my eyes flipped back to the door. I corrected instantly, but his glare had moved on. I wondered if he'd noticed my slip. Or had he seen me at all, here beside Fred?

"We have an enemy," Riley announced. He let that sink in for a moment. I could tell the idea was shocking to several of the vampires in the basement. The enemy was Raoul—or if you were with Raoul, the enemy was Kristie. The enemy was here, because the whole world was here. The thought that there were other forces out there strong enough to affect us was new for most. Would have been new to me, too, yesterday.

"A few of you might be smart enough to have realized that if we exist, so do other vampires. Other vampires who are older, smarter . . . more talented. Other vampires who *want our blood*!"

Raoul hissed, and then several of his followers echoed him in support.

"That's right," Riley said, seeming intent on egging them on. "Seattle was once theirs, but they moved on a long time ago. Now they know about us, and they are jealous of the easy blood they used to have here. They know it belongs to us now, but they want to take it back. They are coming after what they want. One by one, they'll hunt us down! We'll burn while they feast!"

"Never," Kristie growled. Some of hers and some of Raoul's growled, too.

"We don't have a lot of choices," Riley told us. "If we wait for them to show up here, they will have the advantage. This is their turf, after all. And they don't want to face us head-on, because we outnumber them and we are stronger than they are. They want to catch us separated; they want to take advantage of our biggest weakness. Are any of you smart enough to know what that is?" He pointed at the ashes at his feet—now smeared into the carpet and unrecognizable as a former vampire—and waited.

No one moved.

Riley made a disgusted sound. "Unity!" he shouted. "We don't have it! What kind of a threat can we pose when we won't stop killing each other?" He kicked the dust, sending up a small black cloud. "Can you imagine them laughing at us? They think taking the city from us will be easy. That we're weak with stupidity! That we'll just hand them our blood."

Half the vampires in the room snarled in protest now.

"Can you work together, or do we all die?"

"We can take them, boss," Raoul growled.

Riley scowled at him. "Not if you can't control yourself! Not if you can't cooperate with every single person in this room. Anyone you take out"—his toe nudged the ashes again—"might be the one who could have kept you alive. Every one of your coven that you kill is like handing our enemies a gift. *Here*, you're saying, *take me down!*"

Kristie and Raoul exchanged a glance as if they were seeing each other for the first time. Others did the same. The word *coven* was not unfamiliar, but none of us had applied it to our group before. We were a coven.

"Let me tell you about our enemies," Riley said, and all eyes locked on his face. "They are a much older coven than we are. They've been around for hundreds of years, and they've survived that long for a reason. They are crafty and they are skilled and they are coming to retake Seattle with confidence— because they've heard the only ones they'll have to fight for it are a bunch of disorganized children who will do half their work for them!"

More growls, but some were less angry than they were wary. A few of the quieter vampires, the ones Riley would have called *tamer*, looked skittish.

Riley noticed that, too. "This is how they see us, but that's because they can't see us *together*. Together, we can *crush* them. If they could see all of us, side by side, fighting together, they would be terrified. And that's how they're going to see us. Because we're not going to wait for them to show up here and start picking us off. We're going to ambush them. In four days."

Four days? I guessed our creator didn't want to cut it too close to the deadline. I looked at the closed door again. Where was Diego?

Others reacted to the deadline with surprise, some with fear.

"It's the last thing they'll expect," Riley assured us. "All of us—*together*—waiting for them. And I've saved the best part for last. There are only *seven* of them."

There was an instant of incredulous silence.

Then Raoul said, *"What?"*

Kristie stared at Riley with the same disbelieving expression, and I heard muttered whispers around the room.

"Seven?"

"Are you kidding me?"

"Hey," Riley snapped. "I wasn't joking when I said this coven is dangerous. They are wise and . . . devious. Underhanded. We will have power on our side; they will have deception. If we play it their way, they *will* win. But if we take it to them on our terms . . ." Riley didn't finish, he just smiled.

"Let's go now," Raoul urged. "Let's get 'em out of the picture fast." Kevin growled enthusiastically.

"Slow down, moron. Rushing into things blind isn't going to help us win," Riley chided him.

"Tell us everything we need to know about them,"

Kristie encouraged, shooting Raoul a superior look.

Riley hesitated, as if deciding how to word something. "All right, where to begin? I guess the first thing you need to know is . . . that you don't know everything there is to know about vampires yet. I didn't want to overwhelm you in the beginning." Another pause while everyone looked confused. "You have a little bit of experience with what we call 'talents.' We have Fred."

Everyone looked at Fred—or rather they tried to. I could tell from Riley's expression that Fred did not like being singled out. It looked like Fred had really turned up the volume on his "talent," as Riley called it. Riley cringed and looked away quickly. I still didn't feel anything.

"Yes, well, there are some vampires who have gifts beyond the usual super strength and super senses. You've seen one aspect in . . . our coven." He was careful not to say Fred's name again. "Gifts are rare—one in fifty, maybe—but every one is different. There's a huge range of gifts out there, and some of them are more powerful than others."

I could hear a lot of murmurs now as people wondered if they might be talented. Raoul was preening like he'd already decided he was gifted. As far as I could tell, the only one around here that was in any way special was standing next to me.

"Pay attention!" Riley commanded. "I'm not telling you this for entertainment."

"This enemy coven," Kristie interjected. "They're talented. Right?"

Riley gave her an approving nod. "Exactly. I'm glad someone here can connect the dots."

Raoul's upper lip twitched back over his teeth.

"This coven is dangerously talented," Riley went on, his voice dropping to a hushed whisper. "They have a mind reader." He examined our faces, looking to see if we got the importance of this revelation. He didn't seem satisfied with his assessment. *Think*, guys! He'll know everything in your head. If you attack, he'll know what move you're going to make before *you* know it. You go left, he'll be waiting."

There was a nervous stillness as everyone imagined this.

"This is why we've been so careful—me, and the one who created you."

Kristie flinched away from Riley when he mentioned *her*. Raoul looked angrier. Nerves strained universally.

"You don't know her name, and you don't know what she looks like. This protects us all. If they'd stumbled across one of you alone, they wouldn't realize that you were connected to her, and they might have let you be. If they knew you were part of her coven, there would be no delay in your execution."

That didn't make sense to me. Didn't the secrecy protect *her* more than it protected any of us? Riley hurried on before we had too long to examine his statement.

"Of course, it doesn't matter now that they've decided to move on Seattle. We will surprise them on their way in, and we will annihilate them." He whistled a single low note through his teeth. "Done. And then not only is the city all ours, other covens will know not to mess with us. We won't have to be so careful to cover our tracks anymore. As much blood as you want, for everyone. Hunting every night. We'll move right into the city, and *we will rule it*."

The growls and snarls were like applause. Everyone was with him. Except for me. I didn't move, didn't make a sound. Neither did Fred, but who knows why that was?

I was not with Riley because his promises sounded like lies. Or else my whole line of logic had been wrong. Riley said it was only these enemies that kept us from hunting without caution or restraint. But that didn't go along with the fact that all other vampires must have been discreet, or humans would have known about them long ago.

I couldn't concentrate to work it out, because

the door at the top of the stairs had not moved. Diego . . .

"We have to do this together, though. Today I'm going to lead you through some techniques. Fighting techniques. There's more to this than just scuffling around on the floor like toddlers. When it gets dark, we'll go outside and practice. I want you to practice hard, but keep your focus. I am not losing another member of this coven! We all need each other—every one of us. I will not tolerate any more stupidity. If you think you don't have to listen to me, you are wrong." He paused for a short second, the muscles in his face shifting into a new arrangement. "And you will learn how wrong you are when I take you to *her*"—I shuddered and felt the tremor through the room as everyone else did, too—"and hold you while she tears off your legs and then slowly, *slowly* burns off your fingers, ears, lips, tongue, and every other superfluous appendage *one by one*."

We'd all lost a limb, at least, and we'd all burned when we became vampires, so we could easily imagine how that would feel, but it wasn't the threat itself that was so terrifying. The truly scary thing was Riley's face as he said it. His face was not twisted in rage, the way it usually was when he was angry; it was calm and cold, smooth and beautiful, his mouth curled at the edges into a small smile. I suddenly had the impression that this was a new Riley. Something had changed him, hardened him, but I couldn't imagine what could have happened in one night to create that cruel, perfect smile.

I looked away, shivering a little, and saw as Raoul's smile shifted to echo Riley's. I could almost see the gears turning in Raoul's head. He wouldn't kill his victims so quickly in the future.

"Now, let's get some teams figured out so that we can work in groups," Riley said, his face normal again. "Kristie, Raoul, get your kids together and then divvy up the rest evenly. No fighting! Show me you can do this rationally. Prove yourselves."

He walked away from those two, ignoring the fact that they fell almost immediately into bickering, and made an arc around the outside edge of the room. He touched a few vampires on the shoulder as he passed, nudging them toward one of the new leaders or the other. I didn't realize at first that he was heading in my direction, because he took such a wide way around.

"Bree," he said, squinting toward where I stood. It looked like this took some effort.

I felt like a block of ice. He must have smelled my trail. I was dead.

"Bree?" he said, softer now. His voice reminded me of the first time he'd talked to me. When he was nice to me. And then even lower, "I promised Diego I'd give you a message. He said to tell you it was a ninja thing. Does that make any sense to you?"

He still couldn't look at me, but he was edging closer.

"Diego?" I murmured. I couldn't help myself.

Riley smiled a tiny bit. "Can we talk?" He jerked his head toward the door. "I double-checked all the windows. The first floor is totally dark and safe."

I knew I wouldn't be as safe once I walked away from Fred, but I had to hear what Diego had wanted to tell me. What had happened? I should have stayed with him to meet Riley.

I followed Riley through the room, keeping my head down. He gave Raoul a few instructions, nodded to Kristie, and then went up the stairs. From the corners of my eyes I saw a few people curiously watch the direction he was going.

Riley passed through the door first, and the kitchen of the home was, as he'd promised, totally black. He motioned for me to keep following and led me through a dark hall past a few open bedroom doors, then through another door with a dead bolt. We ended up in the garage.

"You're brave," he commented in a very low voice. "Or really trusting. I thought it would be more work to get you upstairs with the sun up."

Whoops. I should have been more skittish. Too late now. I shrugged.

"So you and Diego are pretty tight, right?" he asked, just breathing the words. Probably, if everyone were silent in the basement, they would still be able to hear him, but it was pretty noisy down there right now.

I shrugged again. "He saved my life," I whispered.

Riley lifted his chin, almost but not quite a nod, and appraised. Did he believe me? Did he think I still feared the day?

"He's the best," Riley said. "The smartest kid I've got."

I nodded once.

"We had a little meeting about the situation. We agreed that we need some surveillance. Going in blind is too dangerous. He's the only one I trust to scout ahead." He exhaled, almost angrily. "Wish I had two of him! Raoul's got too short a fuse and Kristie is too self-absorbed to get the big picture, but they're the best I've got, and I'll have to make do. Diego said you were smart, too."

I waited, not sure how much of our story Riley knew.

"I need your help with Fred. Wow, that kid is strong! I couldn't even look at him tonight."

I nodded cautiously again.

"Imagine if our enemies can't even look at us. It will be so *easy*!"

I didn't think Fred would like that idea, but maybe I was wrong. He didn't seem like he cared anything for this coven of ours. Would he want to save us? I didn't respond to Riley.

"You spend a lot of time with him."

I shrugged. "Nobody bothers me there. It's not easy."

Riley pursed his lips and nodded. "Smart, like Diego said."

"Where is Diego?"

I shouldn't have asked. The words just ripped out of their own accord. I waited anxiously, trying to look indifferent and most likely failing.

"We don't have time to waste. I sent him south the second I found out what was coming. If our enemies decide to attack early, we need the advance warning. Diego will meet up with us when we move against them."

I tried to imagine where Diego was now. I wished I were there with him. Maybe I could talk him out of doing Riley's bidding and putting himself in the line of fire in the process. But maybe not. It seemed like Diego was thick with Riley, just like I'd worried.

"Diego wanted me to tell you something."

My eyes snapped to his face. Too fast, too eager. Blew it again.

"Sounded like nonsense to me. He said, 'Tell Bree I've got the handshake figured out. I'll show her in four days, when we meet up.' I have no idea what that means. Do you?"

I tried to force a poker face. "Maybe. He did say something about needing a secret handshake. For his underwater cave. Some kind of password. He was just kidding around, though. I'm not sure what he means now."

Riley chuckled. "Poor Diego."

"What?"

"I think that kid likes you a lot more than you like him."

"Oh." I looked away, confused. Was Diego giving me this message as a way to let me know I could trust Riley? But he hadn't told Riley I knew about the sun. Still, he must have trusted Riley to tell him so much, to show Riley that he cared about me. I thought it would be wiser to keep my mouth shut, though. Too much had changed.

"Don't write him off yet, Bree. He's the best, like I said. Give him a chance."

Riley was giving me romantic advice? This could not get weirder. I bobbed my head once and muttered, "Sure."

"See if you can talk to Fred. Make sure he's on board."

I shrugged. "I'll do what I can."

Riley smiled. "Great. I'll pull you aside before we leave, and you can tell me how it went. I'll keep it casual, not like tonight. I don't want him to feel like I'm spying on him."

"Okay."

Riley motioned for me to follow and then headed back to the basement.

The training lasted all day, but I wasn't part of it. After Riley went back to his team leaders, I took my spot beside Fred. The others had been divided up into four groups of four, with Raoul and Kristie directing them. No one had picked Fred for a side, or maybe he'd ignored them, or maybe they couldn't even see that he was there. I could still see him. He stood out—the only one not participating, a big blond elephant in the room.

I had no desire to insinuate myself into either Raoul's team or Kristie's, so I just watched. No one seemed to notice that I was sitting out with Fred. Though we must have been somewhat invisible, thanks to talented Fred, I felt horribly obvious. I wished I were invisible to *myself*—that I could see the illusion so that I could trust it. But no one noticed us, and after a while I could almost relax.

I watched the practicing closely. I wanted to know everything, just in case. I wasn't planning on fighting; I was planning on finding Diego and making a break for it. But what if Diego wanted to fight? Or what if we had to fight to get away from the rest? Better to pay attention.

Only once did anyone ask about Diego. It was Kevin, but I had a sense that Raoul had put him up to it.

"So, did Diego end up getting fried after all?" Kevin asked in a forced joking tone.

"Diego's with *her*," Riley said, and no one had to ask who he meant. "Surveillance."

A few people shuddered. No one said anything more about Diego.

Was he really with *her*? I cringed at the thought. Maybe Riley was just saying that to keep people from questioning him. He probably didn't want Raoul getting jealous and feeling second best when Riley needed him at his most arrogant today. I couldn't be sure, and I wasn't going to ask. I kept quiet, as usual, and watched the training.

In the end, watching was boring, thirsty work. Riley didn't give his army a break for three days and two nights straight. During the daytime it was harder to stay out of the mix—we all were crammed so tightly into the basement. It made things easier in one way for Riley—he could usually catch a fight before it got ugly. Outside at night, they had more room to really work around each other, but Riley was kept busy darting back and forth to catch limbs and get them back to their owners quickly. He kept his temper well, and he'd been smart enough to find all the lighters this time. I would have bet that this would spin out of control, that we'd lose at least a couple of coven members with Raoul and Kristie skirmishing head to head for days on end. But Riley had better control of them than I had thought possible.

Still, it was mostly repetition. I noticed Riley saying the same things over and over and over again. *Work together, watch your back, don't go at her head-on; work together, watch your back, don't go at him head-on; work together, watch your back, don't go at her head-on.* It was kind of ridiculous, really, and made the group seem exceptionally stupid. But I was sure I would have been just as stupid if I'd been in the thick of the fight with them rather than watching calmly from the sidelines with Fred.

It reminded me in a way of how Riley had drilled into us our fear of the sun. Constant repetition.

Still, it was so dull that after about ten hours that first day, Fred produced a deck of cards and started playing solitaire. That was more interesting than watching the same mistakes over and over again, so I mostly watched him.

After about another twelve hours—we were inside again—I nudged Fred to point out a red five that he could move over. He nodded and made the change. After that hand, he dealt out the cards to both of us, and we played rummy. We never spoke, but Fred smiled a few times. No one ever looked our way or asked us to join in.

There were no hunting breaks, and as time went on, this got harder and harder to ignore. Fights broke out more regularly and with less provocation. Riley's commands got more shrill, and he tore off two arms himself. I tried to forget the burning thirst as much as possible—after all, Riley must have been getting thirsty, too, so this couldn't last forever—but mostly thirst was the only thing on my mind. Fred was looking pretty strained.

Early into the third night—one more day to go, and when I thought about the ticking clock it tied my empty stomach into knots—Riley called all the mock fights to a halt.

"Round it up, kids," he told us, and everyone moved into a loose half-circle facing him. The original gangs all stood close together, so the practicing hadn't changed any of those alliances. Fred put the cards in his back pocket and stood up. I stood close to his side, counting on his repulsive aura to hide me.

"You've done well," Riley told us. "Tonight, you get a reward. Drink up, because tomorrow you're going to want your strength."

Snarls of relief from almost everyone.

"I say *want* and not *need* for a reason," Riley went on. "I think you guys have got this. You've stayed smart and worked hard. Our enemies aren't going to know what's hit them!"

Kristie and Raoul growled, and both of their companies followed suit immediately. I was surprised to see it, but they did look like an army in that moment. Not that they were marching in formation or anything, but there was just something uniform about the response. Like they all were part of one big organism. As always, Fred and I were the glaring exceptions, but I thought only Riley was even the slightest bit aware of us—every now and then his eyes would scan across where we were standing, almost like he was checking to make sure he still felt Fred's talent. And Riley didn't seem to mind that we weren't joining up. For now, anyway.

"Um, you mean tomorrow *night*, right, boss?" Raoul clarified.

"Right," Riley said with a strange little smile. It didn't seem like anyone else noticed anything off in his reply—except for Fred. He looked down at me with one eyebrow raised. I shrugged.

"You ready for your reward?" Riley asked.

His little army roared in response.

"Tonight you get a taste of what our world will be like when our competition is out of the picture. Follow me!"

Riley bounded away; Raoul and his team were right on his heels. Kristie's group started shoving and clawing right through the middle of them to get to the front.

"Don't make me change my mind!" Riley bellowed from the trees ahead. "You can all go thirsty. I don't care!"

Kristie barked an order and her group sullenly fell behind Raoul's. Fred and I waited until the last of them was out of sight. Then Fred did one of those little *ladies first* sweeps with his arm. It didn't feel like he was afraid to have me at his back, just that he was being polite. I started running after the army.

The others were already long gone, but it was nothing to follow their smell. Fred and I ran in companionable silence. I wondered what he was thinking. Maybe he was only thirsty. I was burning, so he probably was, too.

We caught up to the others after about five minutes, but kept our distance. The army was moving in amazing quiet. They were focused, and more . . . disciplined. I kind of wished that Riley had started the training sooner. It was easier to be around this group.

We crossed over an empty two-lane freeway, another strip of forest, and then we were on a beach. The water was smooth, and we'd gone almost due north, so this must have been the strait. We hadn't passed near any residences, and I was sure that was on purpose. Thirsty and on edge, it wouldn't take too much to dissolve this small measure of organization into a screaming free-for-all.

We'd never hunted all together before, and I was pretty sure that it was not a good idea now. I remembered Kevin and the Spider-Man kid fighting over the woman in the car that first night I'd talked to Diego. Riley had better have a whole lot of bodies for us or people were going to start tearing each other up to get the most blood.

Riley paused at the water's edge.

"Don't hold back," he told us. "I want you well fed and strong—at your peak. Now . . . let's go have some fun."

He dove smoothly into the surf. The others were growling excitedly as they submerged, too. Fred and I followed more closely than before because we couldn't follow their scent under water. But I could feel that Fred was hesitant—ready to bolt if this was something other than an all-you-can-eat smorgasbord. It seemed like he didn't trust Riley any more than I did.

We didn't swim long, and then we saw the others kicking upward. Fred and I surfaced last, and Riley started talking as soon as our heads were out of the water, like he'd been waiting for us. He must have been more aware of Fred than the others were.

"There she is," he said, waving toward a large ferry chugging south, probably making the last commuter run of the night down from Canada. "Give me a minute. When the power goes out, she's all yours."

There was an excited murmur. Someone giggled. Riley was off like a shot, and seconds later we saw him fly up the side of the big boat. He headed straight for the control tower on top of the ship. Silencing the radio was my bet. He could say all he wanted about these enemies being our reason for caution, but I was sure there was more to it than that. Humans weren't supposed to know about vampires. At least, not for very long. Just long enough for us to kill them.

Riley kicked a big plate-glass window out of his way and disappeared into the tower. Five seconds later, the lights went out.

I realized Raoul was already gone. He must have

submerged so we wouldn't hear him swimming after Riley. Everyone else took off, and the water churned as if an enormous school of barracuda were attacking.

Fred and I swam at a relatively leisurely pace behind them. In a funny way, it was like we were some old married couple. We never talked, but we still did things at exactly the same time.

We got to the boat about three seconds later, and already the air was full of shrieks and the warm scent of blood. The smell made me realize exactly how thirsty I was, but that was the last thing I realized. My brain shut down completely. There was nothing but fiery pain in my throat and the delicious blood—blood everywhere—promising to put that fire out.

When it was over and there wasn't a heart left beating on the whole ship, I wasn't sure how many people I'd personally killed. More than triple the number I'd ever had on a hunting trip before, easy. I felt hot and flushed. I'd drunk long past the point at which my thirst was totally slaked, just for the taste of the blood. Most of the blood on the ferry was clean and luscious—these passengers had not been dregs. Though I hadn't held back, I was probably at the low end of the kill count. Raoul was so surrounded by mangled bodies that they actually made a little hill. He sat on top of his pile of the dead and laughed loudly to himself.

He wasn't the only one laughing. The dark boat was full of sounds of delight. I heard Kristie say, "That was amazing—three cheers for Riley!" Some of her crowd put up a raucous chorus of hurrahs like a bunch of happy drunks.

Jen and Kevin swung onto the view deck, dripping wet. "Got 'em all, boss," Jen called to Riley. So some people must have tried to swim for it. I hadn't noticed.

I looked around for Fred. It took me a while to find him. I finally realized that I couldn't look directly at the back corner by the vending machines, and I headed that way. At first I felt like the rocking ferry was making me seasick, but then I got close enough that the feeling faded and I could see Fred standing by the window. He smiled at me quickly, and then looked over my head. I followed his gaze and saw that he was watching Riley. I got the feeling that he'd been doing this for some time.

"Okay, kids," Riley said. "You've had a taste of the sweet life, but now we've got work to do!"

They all roared enthusiastically.

"I've got three last things to tell you—and one of those things involves a little dessert—so let's sink this scow and get home!"

With laughter mixed in with the snarls, the army went to work dismantling the boat. Fred and I bailed out the window and watched the demo from a short distance. It didn't take long for the ferry to crumple in the middle with a loud groan of metal. The midsection went down first, with both the bow and the stern twisting up to point to the sky. They sank one at a time, the stern beating the bow by a few seconds. The school of barracuda headed toward us. Fred and I started swimming for shore.

We ran home with the others—though keeping our distance. A couple of times Fred looked at me like he had something he wanted to say, but each time he seemed to change his mind.

Back at the house, Riley let the celebratory mood wind down. Even after a few hours had passed, he still had his hands full trying to get everyone serious again. For once it wasn't a fight he was trying to defuse, just high spirits. If Riley's promises were false, as I thought, he was going to have an issue when the ambush was over. Now that all these vampires had really feasted, they weren't going to go back to any measure of restraint very easily. For tonight, though, Riley was a hero.

Finally—a while after I would have guessed that the sun was up outside—everyone was quiet and paying attention. From their faces, it seemed they were ready to hear just about anything he had to say.

Riley stood halfway up the stairs, his face serious.

"Three things," he began. "First, we want to be sure we get the right coven. If we accidentally run across another clan and slaughter them, we'll tip our hand. We want our enemies overconfident and unprepared. There are two things that mark this coven, and they're pretty hard to miss. One, they look different—they have yellow eyes."

There was a murmur of confusion.

"Yellow?" Raoul repeated in a disgusted tone.

"There's a lot of the vampire world out there that you haven't encountered yet. I told you these vampires were old. Their eyes are weaker than ours—yellowed with age. Another advantage to our side." He nodded to himself as if to say, *one down*. "But other old vampires exist, so there is another way that we'll know them for sure . . . and this is where the dessert I mentioned comes into play." Riley smiled slyly and waited a beat. "This is going to be hard to process," he warned. "I don't understand it, but I've seen it for myself. These old vampires have gone so *soft* that they actually keep—as a member of their coven—a pet human."

His revelation was met by blank silence. Total disbelief.

"I know—hard to swallow. But it's true. We'll

know it's definitely them because a human girl will be with them."

"Like . . . how?" Kristie asked. "You mean they carry meals around with them or something?"

"No, it's always the same girl, just the one, and they don't plan to kill her. I don't know how they manage it, or why. Maybe they just like to be different. Maybe they want to show off their self-control. Maybe they think it makes them look stronger. It makes no sense to me. But I've seen her. More than that, I've smelled her."

Slow and dramatic, Riley reached into his jacket and pulled out a small ziplock bag with red fabric wadded up inside.

"I've done some recon in the past few weeks, checking the yellow-eyes out as soon as they got near the area." He paused to throw us a paternal look. "I watch out for my kids. Anyway, when I could tell that they were moving on us, I grabbed this"—he brandished the bag—"to help us track them. I want you all to get a lock on this scent."

He handed the bag to Raoul, who opened the plastic zipper and inhaled deeply. He glanced up at Riley with a startled look.

"I know," Riley said. "Amazing, right?"

Raoul handed the bag to Kevin, his eyes narrowing in thought.

One by one, each vampire sniffed the bag, and everyone reacted with wide eyes but little else. I was curious enough that I sidled away from Fred until I could feel a hint of the nausea and knew I was outside his circle. I crept forward until I was next to the Spider-Man kid, who seemed to be at the tail end of the line. He sniffed inside the bag when it was his turn and then seemed about to hand it back to the kid who had given it to him, but I held my hand out and hissed quietly. He did a double take—almost like he'd never see me before—and handed me the bag.

It looked like the red fabric was a shirt. I stuck my nose in the opening, keeping my eyes on the vampires near me, just in case, and inhaled.

Ah. I understood the expressions now and felt a similar one on my face. Because the human who had worn this shirt had seriously sweet blood. When Riley said *dessert*, he was dead right. On the other hand, I was less thirsty than I'd ever been. So while my eyes widened in appreciation, I didn't feel enough pain in my throat to make me grimace. It would be awesome to taste this blood, but in that exact moment, it didn't hurt me that I couldn't.

I wondered how long it would take for me to get thirsty again. Usually, a few hours after feeding, the pain would start to come back, and then it would just get worse and worse until—after a couple of days—it was impossible to ignore it even for a second. Would the excessive amount of blood I'd just drunk delay that? I guessed I'd see pretty soon.

I glanced around to make sure no one was waiting for the bag, because I thought Fred would probably be curious, too. Riley caught my eye, smiled the tiniest bit, and jerked his chin slightly toward the corner where Fred was. Which made me want to do the exact opposite of what I'd just been planning, but whatever. I didn't want Riley to be suspicious of me.

I walked back to Fred, ignoring the nausea until it faded and I was right next to him. I handed him the bag. He seemed pleased I'd thought to include him; he smiled and then sniffed the shirt. After a second he nodded thoughtfully to himself. He gave me the bag back with a significant look. The next time we were alone, I thought he would say aloud whatever it was he had seemed to want to share before.

I tossed the bag toward Spider-Man, who reacted like it had fallen out of the sky but still caught it before it hit the ground.

Everyone was buzzing about the scent. Riley clapped his hands together twice.

"Okay, so there's the dessert I was talking about. The girl will be with the yellow-eyes. And whoever gets to her first gets dessert. Simple as that."

Appreciative growls, competitive growls.

Simple, yes, but . . . wrong. Weren't we supposed to be destroying the yellow-eyed coven? Unity was supposed to be the key, not a first-come, first-served prize that only one vampire could win. The only guaranteed outcome from this plan was one dead human. I could think of half a dozen more productive ways to motivate this army. The one who kills the most yellow-eyes wins the girl. The one who shows the best team cooperation gets the girl. The one who sticks to the plan best. The one who follows orders best. MVP, etc. The focus should be on the danger, which was definitely not the human.

I looked around at the others and decided that none of them were following the same train of thought. Raoul and Kristie were glaring at each other. I heard Sara and Jen arguing in whispers about the possibility of sharing the prize.

Well, maybe Fred got it. He was frowning, too.

"And the last thing," Riley said. For the first time there was some reluctance in his voice. "This will probably be even harder to accept, so I'll show you. I won't ask you to do anything I won't do. Remember that—I'm with you guys every step of the way."

The vampires got real still again. I noticed that Raoul had the ziplock back and was gripping it possessively.

"There are so many things you have yet to learn about being a vampire," Riley said. "Some of them make more sense than others. This is one of those things that won't sound right at first, but I've experienced it myself, and I'll show you." He deliberated for a long second. "Four times a year, the sun shines at a certain indirect angle. During that one day, four times a year, it is safe . . . for us to be outside in the daylight."

Every tiny movement stopped. There was no breathing. Riley was talking to a bunch of statues.

"One of those special days is beginning now. The sun that is rising outside today won't hurt any of us. And we are going to use this rare exception to surprise our enemies."

My thoughts spun around and turned upside down. So Riley knew it was safe for us to go out in the sun. Or he didn't, and our creator had told him this "four days a year" story. Or . . . this was true and Diego and I had lucked into one of those days. Except that Diego had been out in the shade before. And Riley was making this into some kind of solstice-y seasonal thing, while Diego and I had been safe in the daylight just four days ago.

I could understand that Riley and our creator would want to control us with the fear of the sun. It made sense. But why tell the truth—in a very limited way—now?

I would bet it had to do with those scary dark-cloaks. She probably wanted to get a jump on her deadline. The cloaked ones had not promised to let her live when we killed all the yellow-eyes. I guessed she would be off like a shot the second she'd accomplished her objective here. Kill the yellow-eyes and then take an extended vacation in Australia or somewhere else on the other side of the world. And I'd bet she wasn't going to send us engraved invitations. I would have to get to Diego quick so we could bail, too. In the opposite direction from Riley and our creator. And I ought to tip Fred off. I decided I would as soon as we had a moment alone.

There was so much manipulation going on in this one little speech, and I wasn't sure I was catching it all. I wished Diego were here so we could analyze it together.

If Riley was just making up this four-days story on the spot, I guess I could understand why. It's not like he could have just said, *Hey, so I've lied to you for your whole lives, but* now *I'm telling the truth.* He wanted us to follow him into battle today; he couldn't undermine whatever trust he'd earned.

"It's right for you to be terrified at the thought," Riley told the statues. "The reason you are all still alive is that you paid attention when I told you to be careful. You got home on time, you didn't make mistakes. You let that fear make you smart and cautious. I don't expect you to put that intelligent fear aside easily. I don't expect you to run out that door on my word. But . . ." He looked around the room once. "I do expect you to *follow* me out."

His eyes slid away from the audience for just the teensiest fraction of a second, touching very briefly on something over my head.

"Watch me," he told us. "Listen to me. Trust me. When you see that I'm okay, believe your eyes. The sun on this one day does have some interesting effects on our skin. You'll see. It won't hurt you in any way. I wouldn't do anything to put you guys in unnecessary danger. You know that."

He started up the stairs.

"Riley, can't we just wait—," Kristie began.

"Just pay attention," Riley cut her off, still moving up at a measured pace. "This gives us a big advantage. The yellow-eyes know all about this day, but they don't know that *we* know." As he was talking, he opened the door and walked out of the basement into the kitchen. There was no light in the well-shaded kitchen, but everyone still shied away from the open doorway. Everyone but me. His voice continued, moving toward the front door. "It takes most young vampires a while to embrace this exception—for good reason. Those who aren't cautious about the daylight don't last long."

I felt Fred's eyes on me. I glanced over at him. He was staring at me urgently, as if he wanted to take off but had nowhere to go.

"It's okay," I whispered almost silently. "The sun's not going to hurt us."

You trust him? he mouthed back at me.

No way.

Fred raised an eyebrow and relaxed just slightly.

I glanced behind us. What had Riley been looking at? Nothing had changed—just some family pictures of dead people, a small mirror, and a cuckoo clock. Hmm. Was he checking the time? Maybe our creator had given him a deadline, too.

"'Kay, guys, I'm going out," Riley said. "You don't have to be afraid today, I promise."

The light burst into the basement through the open door, magnified—as only I knew—by Riley's skin. I could see the bright reflections dance on the wall.

Hissing and snarling, my coven backed into the corner opposite from Fred's. Kristie was in the very back. It looked like she was trying to use her gang as a kind of shield.

"Relax, everybody," Riley called down to us. "I am absolutely fine. No pain, no burn. Come and see. C'mon!"

No one moved closer to the door. Fred was crouched against the wall beside me, eyeing the light with panic. I waved my hand a tiny bit to get his attention. He looked up at me and measured my total calm for a second. Slowly he straightened up next to me. I smiled encouragingly.

Everyone else was waiting for the burn to start. I wondered if I had looked that silly to Diego.

"You know," Riley mused from above, "I'm curious to see who is the bravest one of you. I have a good idea who the first person through that door is going to be, but I've been wrong before."

I rolled my eyes. Subtle, Riley.

But of course it worked. Raoul started inching his way toward the stairs almost immediately. For once, Kristie was in no hurry to compete with him for Riley's approval. Raoul snapped his fingers at Kevin, and both he and the Spider-Man kid reluctantly moved to flank him.

"You can hear me. You know I'm not fried. Don't be a bunch of babies! You're *vampires*. Act like it."

Still, Raoul and his buddies couldn't get farther

than the foot of the stairs. None of the others moved. After a few minutes, Riley came back. In the indirect light from the front door, he shimmered just a tiny bit in the doorway.

"Look at me—I'm fine. Seriously! I'm embarrassed for you. C'mere, Raoul!"

In the end, Riley had to grab Kevin—Raoul ducked out of the way as soon as he could see what Riley was thinking—and drag him upstairs by force. I saw the moment when they made it into the sun, when the light brightened from their reflections.

"Tell them, Kevin," Riley ordered.

"I'm okay, Raoul!" Kevin called down. "Whoa. I'm all . . . shiny. This is crazy!" He laughed.

"Well done, Kevin," Riley said loudly.

That did it for Raoul. He gritted his teeth and marched up the stairs. He didn't move fast, but soon he was up there sparkling and laughing with Kevin.

Even from then on, the process took longer than I would have predicted. It was still a one-by-one thing. Riley got impatient. It was more threats than encouragement now.

Fred shot me a look that said, *You knew this?*

Yes, I mouthed.

He nodded and started up the stairs. There were still about ten people, mostly Kristie's group, huddled against the wall. I went with Fred. Better to come out right in the middle. Let Riley read into that what he would.

We could see the shining, disco-ball vampires in the front yard, staring at their hands and each other's faces with rapt expressions. Fred moved into the light without slowing, which I thought was pretty brave, all things considered. Kristie was a better example of how well Riley had indoctrinated us. She clung to what she knew regardless of the evidence in front of her.

Fred and I stood a little space from the others. He examined himself carefully, then looked me over, then stared at the others. It struck me that Fred, though really quiet, was very observant and almost scientific in the way he examined evidence. He'd been evaluating Riley's words and actions all along. How much had he figured out?

Riley had to force Kristie up the stairs, and her gang came with her. Finally we all were out in the sun, most people enjoying how very pretty they were. Riley rounded everyone up for one more quick practice session—mostly, I thought, to get them to focus again. It took them a minute, but everyone started to realize that this was it, and they got quieter and more fierce. I could see that the idea of a real fight—of being not only allowed but *encouraged* to rip and burn—was almost as exciting as hunting. It appealed to people like Raoul and Jen and Sara.

Riley focused on a strategy he'd been trying to drill into them for the last few days—once we'd pinpointed the yellow-eyes' scent, we were going to divide in two and flank them. Raoul would charge them head-on while Kristie attacked from the side. The plan suited both their styles, though I wasn't sure if they were going to be able to follow this strategy in the heat of the hunt.

When Riley called everyone together after an hour of practice, Fred immediately started walking backward toward the north; Riley had the others facing south. I stayed close, though I had no idea what he was doing. Fred stopped when we were a good hundred yards away, in the shade of the spruce trees on the fringe of the forest. No one watched us move away. Fred was eyeing Riley, as if waiting to see if he would notice our retreat.

Riley began speaking. "We leave now. You're strong and you're ready. And you're thirsty for it, aren't you? You can feel the burn. You're ready for dessert."

He was right. All that blood hadn't slowed the return of the thirst at all. In fact, I wasn't sure, but

I thought it might be coming back faster and harder than usual. Maybe overfeeding was counterproductive in some ways.

"The yellow-eyes are coming in slowly from the south, feeding along the way, trying to get stronger," Riley said. "*She*'s been monitoring them, so I know where to find them. She's going to meet us there, with Diego"—he cast a significant glance toward where I'd just been standing, and then a quick frown that disappeared just as quickly—"and we will hit them like a tsunami. We will overwhelm them easily. And then we will celebrate." He smiled. "Someone's going to get a jump on the celebration. Raoul—give me that." Riley held out his hand imperiously. Raoul reluctantly tossed him the bag with the shirt. It seemed like Raoul was trying to lay claim to the girl by hogging her scent.

"Take another whiff, everybody. Let's get focused!"

Focused on the girl? Or the fight?

Riley himself walked the shirt around this time, almost like he wanted to make sure everyone was thirsty. And I could see from the reactions that, like me, the burn was back for them all. The scent of the shirt made them scowl and snarl. It wasn't necessary to give us the scent again; we forgot nothing. So this was probably just a test. Just thinking about the girl's scent had venom pooling in my mouth.

"Are you with me?" Riley bellowed.

Everyone screamed his or her assent.

"Let's take them down, kids!"

It was like the barracuda again, only on land this time.

Fred didn't move, so I stayed with him, though I knew I was wasting time I needed. If I were going to get to Diego and pull him away before the fighting could start, I would need to be near the front of the attack. I looked after them anxiously. I was still younger than most of them—faster.

"Riley won't be able to think of me for about twenty minutes or so," Fred told me, his voice casual and familiar, like we'd had a million conversations in the past. "I've been gauging the time. Even a good distance away, he'll feel sick if he tries to remember me."

"Really? That's cool."

Fred smiled. "I've been practicing, keeping track of the effects. I can make myself totally invisible now. No one can look at me if I don't want them to."

"I've noticed," I said, then paused and guessed, "You're not going?"

Fred shook his head. "Of course not. It's obvious we're not being told what we need to know. I'm not going to be Riley's pawn."

So Fred had figured it out on his own.

"I was going to take off sooner, but then I wanted to talk to you before I left, and there hasn't been a chance till now."

"I wanted to talk to you, too," I said. "I thought you should know that Riley's been lying about the sun. This four-day thing is a total crock. I think Shelly and Steve and the others figured it out, too. And there's a lot more politics going on with this fight than he's told us. More than one set of enemies." I said it fast, feeling with terrible urgency the movement of the sun, the time passing. I had to get to Diego.

"I'm not surprised," Fred said calmly. "And I'm out. I'm going to explore on my own, see the world. Or I *was* going on my own, but then I thought maybe you might want to come, too. You'd be pretty safe with me. No one will be able to follow us."

I hesitated for a second. The idea of safety was hard to resist in that exact moment.

"I've got to get Diego," I said, shaking my head.

He nodded thoughtfully. "I get it. You know, if you're willing to vouch for him, you can bring him along. Seems like sometimes numbers come in handy."

"Yes," I agreed fervently, remembering how vulnerable I'd felt in the tree alone with Diego as the four cloaks had advanced.

He raised an eyebrow at my tone.

"Riley is lying about at least one more important thing," I explained. "Be careful. We aren't supposed to let humans know about us. There are some kind of freaky vampires who stop covens when they get too obvious. I've seen them, and you don't want them to find you. Just keep out of sight in the day, and hunt smart." I looked south anxiously. "I have to hurry!"

He was processing my revelations solemnly. "Okay. Catch up to me if you want. I'd like to hear more. I'll wait for you in Vancouver for one day. I know the city. I'll leave you a trail in . . ." He thought for a second and then chuckled once. "Riley Park. You can follow it to me. But after twenty-four hours I'm taking off."

"I'll get Diego and catch up to you."

"Good luck, Bree."

"Thanks, Fred! Good luck to you, too. I'll see you!" I was already running.

"I hope so," I heard him say behind me.

I sprinted after the scent of the others, flying along the ground faster than I'd ever run before. I was lucky that they must have paused for something— for Riley to yell at them, I was guessing—because I caught them sooner than I should have. Or maybe Riley had remembered Fred and stopped to look for us. They were running at a steady pace when I reached them, semi-disciplined like last night. I tried to slide into the group without drawing attention, but I saw Riley's head flip around once to scan those trailing behind. His eyes zeroed in on me, and then he started running faster. Did he assume Fred was with me? Riley would never see Fred again.

It wasn't five minutes later when everything changed.

Raoul caught the scent. With a wild growl he was off. Riley had us so worked up that it took only the tiniest spark to set off an explosion. The others near Raoul had the scent, too, and then everyone went crazy. Riley's harping on this human had overshadowed the rest of his instructions. We were hunters, not an army. There was no team. It was a race for blood.

Even though I knew there were a lot of lies in the story, I couldn't totally resist the scent. Running at the back of the pack, I had to cross it. Fresh. Strong. The human had been here recently, and she smelled so sweet. I was strong with all the blood we'd drunk last night, but it didn't matter. I was thirsty. It burned.

I ran after the others, trying to keep my head clear. It was all I could do to hold back a little, to stay behind the others. The closest person to me was Riley. He was . . . holding back, too?

He shouted orders, mostly the same thing repeated. "Kristie, go around! Move around! Split off! Kristie, Jen! *Break off!*" His whole plan of the two-pronged ambush was self-destructing as we watched.

Riley sped up to the main group and grabbed Sara's shoulder. She snapped at him as he hurled her to the left. "Go around!" he shouted. He caught the blond kid whose name I'd never figured out and shoved him into Sara, who clearly wasn't happy with that. Kristie came out of the hunting focus long enough to realize she was supposed to be moving strategically. She gave one fierce gaze after Raoul and then started screeching at her team.

"This way! Faster! We'll beat them around and get to her first! C'mon!"

"I'm spear point with Raoul!" Riley shouted at her, turning away.

I hesitated, still running forward. I didn't want to be part of any "spear point," but Kristie's team was already turning on each other. Sara had the blond kid in a headlock. The sound of his head tearing off made my decision for me. I sprinted after Riley, wondering if Sara would pause to burn the boy who liked to play Spider-Man.

I caught up enough to see Riley ahead and fol-lowed at a distance until he got to Raoul's team. The scent made it hard to keep my mind on the things that mattered.

"Raoul!" Riley yelled.

Raoul grunted, not turning. He was totally absorbed by the sweet scent.

"I've got to help Kristie! I'll meet you there! Keep your focus!"

I jerked to a stop, frozen with uncertainty.

Raoul kept on, not showing any response to Riley's words. Riley slowed to a jog, then a walk. I should have moved, but he probably would have heard me try to hide. He turned, a smile on his face, and saw me.

"Bree. I thought you were with Kristie."

I didn't respond.

"I heard someone get hurt—Kristie needs me more than Raoul," he explained quickly.

"Are you . . . leaving us?"

Riley's face changed. It was like I could see his shifting tactics written on his features. His eyes widened, suddenly anxious.

"I'm worried, Bree. I told you that *she* was going to meet us, to help us, but I haven't crossed her trail. Something's wrong. I need to find her."

"But there's no way you can find her before Raoul gets to the yellow-eyes," I pointed out.

"I have to find out what's going on." He sounded genuinely desperate. "I need her. I wasn't supposed to do this alone!"

"But the others . . ."

"Bree, I have to go find her! Now! There are enough of you to overwhelm the yellow-eyes. I'll get back to you as soon as I can."

He sounded so sincere. I hesitated, glancing back the way we had come. Fred would be halfway to Vancouver by now. Riley hadn't even asked about him. Maybe Fred's talent was still in effect.

"Diego's down there, Bree," Riley said urgently. "He'll be part of the first attack. Didn't you catch his scent back there? Did you not get close enough?"

I shook my head, totally confused. "Diego was there?"

"He's with Raoul by now. If you hurry, you can help him get out alive."

We stared at each other for a long second, and then I looked south after Raoul's path.

"Good girl," Riley said. "I'll go find *her* and we'll be back to help clean up. You guys have got this! It might be over by the time you get there!"

He took off in a direction perpendicular to our original path. I clenched my teeth at how sure he seemed of his way. Lying to the end.

But it didn't feel like I had a choice. I headed south in a flat-out sprint again. I had to go get Diego. Drag him away if it came to that. We could catch up with Fred. Or take off on our own. We needed to run. I would tell Diego how Riley had lied. He would see that Riley had no intention of helping us fight the battle he'd set up. There was no reason to help him anymore.

I found the human's scent and then Raoul's. I didn't catch Diego's. Was I going too fast? Or was the human's scent just overpowering me? Half my head was absorbed in this strangely counterproductive hunt—sure, we would find the girl, but would we be ready to fight together when we did? No, we'd be clawing each other apart to get to her.

And then I heard the snarling and screaming and screeching explode from ahead and I knew the fight was happening and I was too late to beat Diego there. I only ran faster. Maybe I could still save him.

I smelled the smoke—the sweet, thick scent of vampires burning—carried back to me on the wind. The sound of mayhem was louder. Maybe it was almost done. Would I find our coven victorious and Diego waiting?

I dashed through a heavy fringe of smoke and found myself out of the forest in a huge grassy field.

I leaped over a rock, only to realize in the instant I flew past it that it was a headless torso.

My eyes raked the field. There were pieces of vampires everywhere, and a huge bonfire smoking purple into the sunny sky. Out from under the billowing haze, I could see dazzling, glittering bodies darting and grappling as the sounds of vampires being torn apart went on and on.

I looked for one thing: Diego's curly black hair. No one I could see had hair so dark. There was one huge vampire with brown hair that was almost black, but he was too big, and as I focused I watched him tear Kevin's head off and pitch it into the fire before leaping on someone else's back. Was that Jen? There was another with straight black hair that was too small to be Diego. That one was moving so fast I couldn't tell if it was a boy or a girl.

I scanned quickly again, feeling horribly exposed. I took in the faces. There weren't nearly enough vampires here, even counting those that were down. I didn't see any of Kristie's group. There must have been a lot of vampires burned already. Most of the vampires still standing were strangers. A blond vampire glanced at me, meeting my gaze, and his eyes flashed gold in the sunlight.

We were losing. Bad.

I started backing toward the trees, not moving

fast enough because I was still looking for Diego. He wasn't here. There was no sign he had ever been here. No trace of his scent, though I could distinguish the smells of most of Raoul's team and many strangers. I had made myself look at the pieces, too. None of them belonged to Diego. I would have recognized even a finger.

I turned and really ran for the trees, suddenly positive that Diego's presence here was just another of Riley's lies.

And if Diego wasn't here, then he was already dead. This fell into place for me so easily that I thought I must have known the truth for a while. Since the moment that Diego had not followed Riley through the basement door. He'd already been gone.

I was a few feet into the trees when a force like a wrecking ball hit me from behind and threw me to the ground. An arm slipped under my chin.

"Please!" I sobbed. And I meant *please kill me fast*.

The arm hesitated. I didn't fight back, though my instincts were urging me to bite and claw and rip the enemy apart. The saner part of me knew that wasn't going to work. Riley had lied about these weak, older vampires, too, and we'd never had a chance. But even if I'd had a way to beat this one, I wouldn't have been able to move. Diego was gone, and that glaring fact killed the fight in me.

Suddenly I was airborne. I crashed into a tree and crumpled to the ground. I should have tried to run, but Diego was dead. I couldn't get around that.

The blond vampire from the clearing was staring intently at me, his body ready to spring. He looked very capable, much more experienced than Riley. But he wasn't lunging at me. He wasn't crazed like Raoul or Kristie. He was totally in control.

"Please," I said again, wanting him to get this over with. "I don't want to fight."

Though he still held himself ready, his face changed. He looked at me in a way I didn't totally get. There was a lot of knowledge in that face, and something else. Empathy? Pity, at least.

"Neither do I, child," he said in a calm, kind voice. "We are only defending ourselves."

There was such honesty in his odd yellow eyes that it made me wonder how I had ever believed any of Riley's stories. I felt . . . guilty. Maybe this coven had never planned to attack us in Seattle. How could I trust any part of what I'd been told?

"We didn't know," I explained, somehow ashamed. "Riley lied. I'm sorry."

He listened for a moment, and I realized that the battlefield was quiet. It was over.

If I'd been in any doubt over who the winner was,

that doubt was gone when, a second later, a female vampire with wavy brown hair and yellow eyes hurried to his side.

"Carlisle?" she asked in a confused voice, staring at me.

"She doesn't want to fight," he told her.

The woman touched his arm. He was still tensed to spring. "She's so frightened, Carlisle. Couldn't we . . ."

The blond, Carlisle, glanced back at her, and then he straightened up a little, though I could see he was still wary.

"We have no wish to harm you," the woman said to me. She had a soft, soothing voice. "We didn't want to fight any of you."

"I'm sorry," I whispered again.

I couldn't make sense of the mess in my head. Diego was dead, and that was the main thing, the devastating thing. Other than that, the fight was over, my coven had lost and my enemies had won. But my dead coven was full of people who would have loved to watch me burn, and my enemies were speaking to me kindly when they had no reason to. Moreover, I felt safer with these two strangers than I'd ever felt with Raoul and Kristie. I was *relieved* that Raoul and Kristie were dead. It was so confusing.

"Child," Carlisle said, "will you surrender to us?

If you do not try to harm us, we promise we will not harm you."

And I believed him.

"Yes," I whispered. "Yes, I surrender. I don't want to hurt anybody."

He held out his hand encouragingly. "Come, child. Let our family regroup for a moment, then we'll have some questions for you. If you answer honestly, you have nothing to fear."

I got up slowly, making no movements that could be considered threatening.

"Carlisle?" a male voice called.

And then another yellow-eyed vampire joined us. Any sort of safety I'd felt with these strangers vanished as soon as I saw him.

He was blond, like the first, but taller and leaner. His skin was absolutely covered in scars, spaced most thickly together on his neck and jaw. A few small marks on his arm were fresh, but the rest were not from the brawl today. He had been in more fights than I could have imagined, and he'd never lost. His tawny eyes blazed and his stance exuded the barely contained violence of an angry lion.

As soon as he saw me he coiled to spring.

"Jasper!" Carlisle warned.

Jasper pulled up short and stared at Carlisle with wide eyes. "What's going on?"

"She doesn't want to fight. She's surrendered."

The scarred vampire's brow clouded, and suddenly I felt an unexpected surge of frustration, though I had no idea what I was frustrated with.

"Carlisle, I . . ." He hesitated, then continued, "I'm sorry, but that's not possible. We can't have any of these newborns associated with us when the Volturi come. Do you realize the danger that would put us in?"

I didn't understand exactly what he was saying, but I got enough. He wanted to kill me.

"Jasper, she's only a child," the woman protested. "We can't just murder her in cold blood!"

It was strange to hear her speak like we both were people, like murder was a bad thing. An avoidable thing.

"It's our family on the line here, Esme. We can't afford to have them think we broke this rule."

The woman, Esme, walked between me and the one who wanted to kill me. Incomprehensibly, she turned her back to me.

"No. I won't stand for it."

Carlisle shot me an anxious glance. I could see that he cared a lot for this woman. I would have looked the same way at anyone behind Diego's back. I tried to appear as docile as I felt.

"Jasper, I think we have to take the chance," he

said slowly. "We are not the Volturi. We follow their rules, but we do not take lives lightly. We will explain."

"They might think we created our own newborns in defense."

"But we didn't. And even had we, there was no indiscretion here, only in Seattle. There is no law against creating vampires if you control them."

"This is too dangerous."

Carlisle touched Jasper's shoulder tentatively. "Jasper. We cannot kill this child."

Jasper glowered at the man with the kind eyes, and I was suddenly angry. Surely he wouldn't hurt this gentle vampire or the woman he loved. Then Jasper sighed, and I knew it was okay. My anger evaporated.

"I don't like this," he said, but he was calmer. "At least let me take charge of her. You two don't know how to deal with someone who's been running wild so long."

"Of course, Jasper," the woman said. "But be kind."

Jasper rolled his eyes. "We need to be with the others. Alice said we don't have long."

Carlisle nodded. He held his hand out to Esme, and they headed past Jasper back toward the open field.

"You there," Jasper said to me, his face a glower

again. "Come with us. Don't make one rash move or I *will* take you down."

I felt angry again as he glared at me, and a small part of me wanted to snarl and show my teeth, but I had a feeling he was looking for just that kind of excuse.

Jasper paused as if he'd just thought of something. "Close your eyes," he commanded.

I hesitated. Had he decided to kill me after all?

"Do it!"

I gritted my teeth and shut my eyes. I felt twice as helpless as I had before.

"Follow the sound of my voice and don't open your eyes. You look, you lose, got it?"

I nodded, wondering what he didn't want me to see. I felt some relief that he was bothering to protect a secret. There was no reason to do so if he was just going to kill me.

"This way."

I walked slowly after him, careful to give him no excuses. He was considerate in the way he led, not walking me into any trees, at least. I could hear the way the sound changed when we were in the open; the feel of the wind was different, too, and the smell of my coven burning was stronger. I could feel the warmth of the sun on my face, and the insides of my eyelids were brighter as I sparkled.

He led me closer and closer to the muffled crackle of the flames, so close that I could feel the smoke brush my skin. I knew he could have killed me at any time, but the nearness of the fire still made me nervous.

"Sit here. Eyes closed."

The ground was warm from the sun and the fire. I kept very still and tried to concentrate on looking harmless, but I could feel his glare on me, and it made me agitated. Though I was not mad at these vampires, who I truly believed had only been defending themselves, I felt the oddest stirrings of fury. It was almost outside myself, as if it were some leftover echo from the battle that had just taken place.

The anger didn't make me stupid, though, because I was too sad—miserable to my core. Diego was aways in my mind, and I couldn't help thinking about how he must have died.

I was sure there was no way he would have voluntarily told Riley our secrets—secrets that had given me a reason to trust Riley just enough until it was too late. In my head, I saw Riley's face again— that cold, smooth expression that had formed as he'd threatened to punish any of us who wouldn't behave. I heard again his macabre and oddly detailed description—*when I take you to her and hold you as she tears off your legs and then slowly, slowly burns off your fingers, ears, lips, tongue, and every other superfluous appendage one by one.*

I realized now that I'd been hearing the description of Diego's death.

That night, I'd been sure that something had changed in Riley. Killing Diego was what had changed Riley, had hardened him. I believed only one thing that Riley had ever told me: he had valued Diego more than any of the rest of us. Had even been fond of him. And yet he'd watched our creator hurt him. No doubt he'd helped her. Killed Diego with her.

I wondered how much pain it would have taken to make me betray Diego. I imagined it would have taken quite a lot. And I was sure it had taken at least that much to make Diego betray me.

I felt sick. I wanted the image of Diego screaming in agony out of my head, but it wouldn't leave.

And then there was screaming there in the field.

My eyelids fluttered, but Jasper snarled furiously and I clenched them together at once. I'd seen nothing but heavy lavender smoke.

I heard shouting and a strange, savage howling. It was loud, and there was a lot of it. I couldn't imagine how a face would have to contort to create such a noise, and the not knowing made the sound more frightening. These yellow-eyed vampires were so different from the rest of us. Or different from *me*, I guess, since I was the only one left. Riley and our creator were long gone by now.

I heard names called, *Jacob*, *Leah*, *Sam*. There were lots of distinct voices, though the howls continued. Of course Riley had lied to us about the number of vampires here, too.

The sound of the howling tapered off until it was just one voice, one agonized, inhuman yowling that made me grit my teeth. I could see Diego's face so clearly in my mind, and the sound was like him screaming.

I heard Carlisle talking over the other voices and the howling. He was begging to look at something. "Please let me take a look. Please let me help." I didn't hear anyone arguing with him, but for some reason his tone made it sound like he was losing the dispute.

And then the yowling reached a strident new pitch, and suddenly Carlisle was saying "thank you" in a fervent voice, and under the yowl there was the sound of a lot of movement by a lot of bodies. Many heavy footsteps coming closer.

I listened harder and heard something unexpected and impossible. Along with some heavy breathing— and I've never heard anyone in my coven breathe like that—there were dozens of deep thumping noises.

Almost like . . . heartbeats. But definitely not human hearts. I knew that particular sound well. I sniffed hard, but the wind was blowing from the other direction, and I could only smell the smoke.

Without a warning sound, something touched me, clapped down firmly on either side of my head.

My eyes started open in panic as I lurched up, straining to jerk free of this hold, and instantly met Jasper's warning gaze about two inches from my face.

"Stop it," he snapped, yanking me back down on my butt. I could only just hear him, and I realized that his hands were sealed tight against my head, covering my ears entirely.

"Close your eyes," he instructed again, probably at a normal volume, but it was hushed for me.

I struggled to calm myself and shut my eyes again. There were things they didn't want me to hear, either. I could live with that—if it meant I could live.

For a second I saw Fred's face behind my eyelids. He had said he would wait for one day. I wondered if he would keep his word. I wished I could tell him the truth about the yellow-eyes, and how much more there seemed to be that we didn't know. This whole world that we really knew nothing about.

It would be interesting to explore that world. Particularly with someone who could make me invisible and safe.

But Diego was gone. He wouldn't be coming to find Fred with me. That made imagining the future faintly repugnant.

I could still hear some of what was going on, but just the howling and a few voices. Whatever those weird thumping sounds had been, they were too muted now for me to examine them.

I did make out the words when, a few minutes later, Carlisle said, "You have to . . ."—his voice was too low for a second, and then—". . . from here now. If we could help we would, but we cannot leave."

There was a growl, but it was oddly unmenacing. The yowling became a low whine that disappeared slowly, as if it was moving away from me.

It was quiet for a few minutes. I heard some low voices, Carlisle and Esme among them, but also some I didn't know. I wished I could smell something—the blindness combined with the muted sound left me straining for some source of sensory information. But all I could smell was the horribly sweet smoke.

There was one voice, higher and clearer than the others, that I could hear most easily.

"Another five minutes," I heard whoever it was

say. I was sure it was a girl who was speaking. "And Bella will open her eyes in thirty-seven seconds. I wouldn't doubt that she can hear us now."

I tried to make sense of this. Was someone else being forced to keep her eyes shut, like me? Or did she think my name was Bella? I hadn't told anyone my name. I struggled again to smell *something*.

More mumbling. I thought that one voice sounded off—I couldn't hear any ring to it at all. But I couldn't be sure with Jasper's hands so securely over my ears.

"Three minutes," the high, clear voice said.

Jasper's hands left my head.

"You'd better open your eyes now," he told me from a few steps away. The way he said this frightened me. I looked around myself quickly, searching for the danger hinted at in his tone.

One whole field of my vision was obscured by the dark smoke. Close by, Jasper was frowning. His teeth were gritted together and he was looking at me with an expression that was almost . . . frightened. Not like he was scared of me, but like he was scared *because* of me. I remembered what he'd said before, about my putting them in danger with something called a Volturi. I wondered what a Volturi was. I couldn't imagine what this scarred-up, dangerous vampire would be afraid of.

Behind Jasper, four vampires were spaced out in

a loose line with their backs to me. One was Esme. With her were a tall blonde woman, a tiny black-haired girl, and a dark-haired male vampire so big that he was scary just to look at—the one I'd seen kill Kevin. For an instant I imagined that vampire getting a hold on Raoul. It was a strangely pleasant picture.

There were three more vampires behind the big one. I couldn't see exactly what they were doing with him in the way. Carlisle was kneeling on the ground, and next to him was a male vampire with dark red hair. Lying flat on the ground was another figure, but I couldn't see much of that one, only jeans and small brown boots. It was either a female or a young male. I wondered if they were putting the vampire back together.

So eight yellow-eyes total, plus all that howling before, whatever strange kind of vampire *that* had been; there had been at least eight more voices involved. Sixteen, maybe more. More than twice as many as Riley had told us to expect.

I found myself fiercely hoping that those black-cloaked vampires would catch up to Riley, and that they would make him *suffer*.

The vampire on the ground started to get slowly to her feet—moving awkwardly, almost like she was some clumsy human.

The breeze shifted, blowing the smoke across me and Jasper. For a moment, everything was invisible except for him. Though I was not as blind as before, I suddenly felt much more anxious, for some reason. It was like I could feel the anxiety bleeding out of the vampire next to me.

The light wind gusted back in the next second, and I could see and smell everything.

Jasper hissed at me furiously and shoved me out of my crouch and back onto the ground.

It was her—the human I'd been hunting just a few minutes ago. The scent my whole body had been focused toward. The sweet, wet scent of the most delicious blood I'd ever tracked. My mouth and throat felt like they were on fire.

I tried wildly to hold on to my reason—to focus on the fact that Jasper was just waiting for me to jump up again so that he could kill me—but only part of me could do it. I felt like I was about to pull into two halves trying to keep myself here.

The human named Bella stared at me with stunned brown eyes. Looking at her made it worse. I could see the blood flushing through her thin skin. I tried to look anywhere else, but my eyes kept circling back to her.

The redhead spoke to her in a low voice. "She surrendered. That's one I've never seen before. Only

Carlisle would think of offering. Jasper doesn't approve."

Carlisle must have explained to that one when my ears were covered.

The vampire had both his arms around the human girl, and she had both hands pressed to his chest. Her throat was just inches from his mouth, but she didn't look frightened of him at all. And he didn't look like he was hunting. I had tried to wrap my head around the idea of a coven with a pet human, but this was not close to what I had imagined. If she'd been a vampire, I would have guessed that they were together.

"Is Jasper all right?" the human whispered.

"He's fine. The venom stings," the vampire said.

"He was bitten?" she asked, sounding shocked by the idea.

Who was this girl? Why did the vampires allow her to be with them? Why hadn't they killed her yet? Why did she seem so comfortable with them, like they didn't scare her? She seemed like she was a part of this world, and yet she didn't understand its realities. Of course Jasper was bitten. He'd just fought—and destroyed—my entire coven. Did this girl even know what we were?

Ugh, the burn in my throat was impossible! I tried not to think about washing it away with her blood, but the wind was blowing her smell right in my face! It was too late to keep my head—I had scented the prey I was hunting, and nothing could change that now.

"He was trying to be everywhere at once," the redhead told the human. "Trying to make sure Alice had nothing to do, actually." He shook his head as he looked at the tiny black-haired girl. "Alice doesn't need anyone's help."

The vampire named Alice shot a glare at Jasper. "Overprotective fool," she said in her clear soprano voice. Jasper met her stare with a half smile, seeming to forget for a second that I existed.

I could barely fight the instinct that wanted me to make use of his lapse and spring at the human girl. It would take less than an instant and then her warm blood—blood I could hear pumping through her heart—would quench the burn. She was so *close*—

The vampire with the dark red hair met my eyes with a fierce warning glare, and I knew I would die if I tried for the girl, but the agony in my throat made me feel like I would die if I didn't. It hurt so much that I screamed out loud in frustration.

Jasper snarled at me, and I tried to keep myself from moving, but it felt like the scent of her blood was a giant hand yanking me off the ground. I had never tried to stop myself from feeding once I had committed to a hunt. I dug my hands into the ground looking for something to hold on to but finding nothing. Jasper leaned into a crouch, and even knowing I was two seconds from death, I couldn't focus my thirsty thoughts.

And then Carlisle was right there, his hand on Jasper's arm. He looked at me with kind, calm eyes. "Have you changed your mind, young one?" he asked me. "We don't want to destroy you, but we will if you can't control yourself."

"How can you stand it?" I asked him, almost begging. Wasn't he burning, too? "I *want* her." I stared at her, desperately wishing the distance between us was gone. My fingers raked uselessly through the rocky dirt.

"You must stand it," Carlisle said solemnly. "You must exercise control. It is possible, and it is the only thing that will save you now."

If being able to tolerate the human the way these strange vampires did was my only hope for survival, then I was already doomed. I couldn't stand the fire. And I was of two minds about survival anyway. I didn't want to die, I didn't want pain, but what was the point? Everyone else was dead. Diego had been dead for days.

His name was right on my lips. I almost whispered

it aloud. Instead, I gripped my skull with both hands and tried to think about something that wouldn't hurt. Not the girl, and not Diego. It didn't work very well.

"Shouldn't we move away from her?" the human whispered roughly, breaking my concentration. My eyes snapped back to her. Her skin was so thin and soft. I could see the pulse in her neck.

"We have to stay here," said the vampire she was clinging to. "*They* are coming to the north end of the clearing now."

They? I glanced to the north, but there was nothing but smoke. Did he mean Riley and my creator? I felt a new thrill of panic, followed by a little spasm of hope. There was no way she and Riley could stand against these vampires who had killed so many of us, was there? Even if the howly ones were gone, Jasper alone looked capable of dealing with the two of them.

Or did he mean this mysterious Volturi?

The wind teased the girl's scent across my face again, and my thoughts scattered. I glared at her thirstily.

The girl met my stare, but her expression was so different from what it should have been. Though I could feel that my lips were curled back from my teeth, though I trembled with the effort to stop myself from springing at her, she did not look afraid of me. Instead she seemed fascinated. It almost looked like she wanted to speak to me—like she had a question she wanted me to answer.

Then Carlisle and Jasper began to back away from the fire—and me—closing ranks with the others and the human. They all were staring past me into the smoke, so whatever they were afraid of was closer to me than it was to them. I huddled tighter to the smoke in spite of the nearby flames. Should I make a run for it? Were they distracted enough that I could escape? Where would I go? To Fred? Off on my own? To find Riley and make him pay for what he'd done to Diego?

As I hesitated, mesmerized by that last idea, the moment passed. I heard movement to the north and knew I was sandwiched between the yellow-eyes and whatever was coming.

"Hmm," a dead voice said from behind the smoke.

In that one syllable I knew exactly who it was, and if I hadn't been frozen solid with mindless terror I would have bolted.

It was the dark-cloaks.

What did this mean? Would a new battle begin now? I knew that the dark-cloaked vampires had wanted my creator to succeed in destroying these yellow-eyes. My creator had clearly failed. Did that mean they would kill her? Or would they kill Carlisle and Esme and the rest here instead? If it had been my choice, I knew who I would want destroyed, and it wasn't my captors.

The dark-cloaks ghosted through the vapor to face the yellow-eyes. None of them looked in my direction. I held absolutely still.

There were only four of them, like last time. But it didn't make a difference that there were seven of the yellow-eyes. I could tell that they were as wary of these dark-cloaks as Riley and my creator had been. There was something more to them than I could see, but I could definitely *feel* it. These were the punishers, and they didn't lose.

"Welcome, Jane," said the yellow-eyed one who held the human.

They knew each other. But the redhead's voice was not friendly—nor was it weak and eager to please like Riley's had been, or furiously terrified like my creator's. His voice was simply cold and polite and unsurprised. Were the dark-cloaks this Volturi, then?

The small vampire who led the dark-cloaks—Jane, apparently—slowly scanned across the seven yellow-eyes and the human, and then finally turned her head toward me. I glimpsed her face for the first time. She was younger than me, but much older, too, I guessed. Her eyes were the velvet color of dark red roses. Knowing it was too late to escape notice, I put my head down, covering it with my hands. Maybe if it were clear that I didn't want to fight, Jane would treat me as Carlisle had. I didn't feel much hope of that, though.

"I don't understand." Jane's dead voice betrayed a hint of annoyance.

"She has surrendered," the redhead explained.

"Surrendered?" Jane snapped.

I peeked up to see the dark-cloaks exchanging glances. The redhead had said that he'd never seen anyone surrender before. Maybe the dark-cloaks hadn't, either.

"Carlisle gave her the option," the redhead said. He seemed to be the spokesperson for the yellow-eyes, though I thought Carlisle might be the leader.

"There are no options for those who break the rules," Jane said, her voice dead again.

My bones felt like ice, but I didn't feel panicked anymore. It all seemed so inevitable now.

Carlisle answered Jane in a soft voice. "That's in your hands. As long as she was willing to halt her attack on us, I saw no need to destroy her. She was never taught."

Though his words were neutral, I almost thought

he was pleading for me. But, as he had said, my fate was not up to him.

"That is irrelevant," Jane confirmed.

"As you wish."

Jane was staring at Carlisle with an expression that was half confusion and half frustration. She shook her head, and her face was unreadable again.

"Aro hoped that we would get far enough west to see you, Carlisle," she said. "He sends his regards."

"I would appreciate it if you would convey mine to him," he answered.

Jane smiled. "Of course." Then she looked at me again, with the corners of her mouth still slightly holding the smile. "It appears that you've done our work for us today . . . for the most part. Just out of professional curiosity, how many were there? They left quite a wake of destruction in Seattle."

She spoke of jobs and professionals. I was right, then, that it was her profession to punish. And if there were punishers, then there must be rules. Carlisle had said before, *We follow their rules*, and also, *There is no law against creating vampires if you control them*. Riley and my creator had been afraid but not exactly surprised by the arrival of the dark-cloaks, these Volturi. They knew about the laws, and they knew they were breaking them. Why hadn't they told us? And there were more Volturi than just these four. Someone named Aro and probably many more. There must have been a lot for everyone to fear them so much.

Carlisle answered Jane's question. "Eighteen, including this one."

There was a barely audible murmur among the four dark-cloaks.

"Eighteen?" Jane repeated, a note of surprise in her voice. Our creator had never told Jane how many of us she'd created. Was Jane really surprised, or just faking it?

"All brand-new," Carlisle said. "They were unskilled."

Unskilled and uninformed, thanks to Riley. I was beginning to get a sense of how these older vampires viewed us. *Newborn*, Jasper had called me. Like a baby.

"All?" Jane snapped. "Then who was their creator?"

As if they hadn't already been introduced. This Jane was a bigger liar than Riley, and she was so much better at it than he was.

"Her name was Victoria," the redhead answered.

How did he know that when even *I* didn't? I remembered that Riley had said there was a mind reader in this group. Was that how they knew everything? Or was that another of Riley's lies?

"Was?" Jane asked.

The redhead jerked his head toward the east like he was pointing. I looked up and saw a cloud of thick lilac smoke billowing from the side of the mountain.

Was. I felt a similar kind of pleasure to what I'd felt imagining the big vampire shredding Raoul. Only much, much greater.

"This Victoria," Jane asked slowly. "She was in addition to the eighteen here?"

"Yes," the redhead confirmed. "She had only one other with her. He was not as young as this one here, but no older than a year."

Riley. My fierce pleasure intensified. If—okay, *when*—I died today, at least I didn't leave that loose thread. Diego had been avenged. I almost smiled.

"Twenty," Jane breathed. Either this was more than she had expected, or she was a killer actress. "Who dealt with the creator?"

"I did," the redhead said coldly.

Whoever this vampire was, whether he kept a pet human or no, he was a friend of mine. Even if he were the one to kill me in the end, I would still owe him.

Jane turned to stare at me with narrowed eyes.

"You there," she snarled. "Your name."

I was dead anyway, according to her. So why give this lying vampire anything she wanted? I just glared at her.

Jane smiled at me, the bright, happy smile of an innocent child, and suddenly I was on fire. It was like I'd gone back in time to the worst night of my life. Fire was in every vein of my body, covering every inch of my skin, gnawing through the marrow of every bone. It felt like I was buried in the middle of my coven's funeral bonfire, with the flames on every side. There wasn't a single cell in my body that wasn't blazing with the worst agony imaginable. I could barely hear myself scream over the pain in my ears.

"Your name," Jane said again, and as she spoke the fire disappeared. Gone like that, as if I'd only been imagining it.

"Bree," I said as fast as I could, still gasping though the pain wasn't there anymore.

Jane smiled again and the fire was everywhere. How much pain would it take before I would die of it? The screams didn't even feel like they were coming from me anymore. Why wouldn't someone rip my head off? Carlisle was kind enough for that, wasn't he? Or whoever their mind reader was. Couldn't he or she understand and *make this stop*?

"She'll tell you anything you want to know," the redhead growled. "You don't have to do that."

The pain vanished again, like Jane had turned

off a light switch. I found myself facedown on the ground, panting as if I needed air.

"Oh, I know," I heard Jane say cheerfully. "Bree?"

I shuddered when she called my name, but the pain didn't start again.

"Is his story true?" she asked me. "Were there twenty of you?"

The words flew out of my mouth. "Nineteen or twenty, maybe more, I don't know! Sara and the one whose name I don't know got in a fight on the way. . . ."

I waited for the pain to punish me for not having a better answer, but instead Jane spoke again.

"And this Victoria—did she create you?"

"I don't know," I admitted fearfully. "Riley never said her name. I didn't see that night . . . it was so dark, and it hurt!" I flinched. "He didn't want us to be able to think of her. He said that our thoughts weren't safe."

Jane shot a glance at the redhead, then looked at me again.

"Tell me about Riley," Jane said. "Why did he bring you here?"

I recited Riley's lies as quickly as I could. "Riley told us that we had to destroy the strange yellow-eyes here. He said it would be easy. He said that the city was theirs, and they were coming to get us. He said once they were gone, all the blood would be ours. He gave us her scent." I pointed in the human's direction. "He said we would know that we had the right coven, because she would be with them. He said whoever got to her first could have her."

"It looks like Riley was wrong about the easy part," Jane said, a hint of teasing in her tone.

It seemed like Jane was pleased with my story. In a flash of insight, I understood that she was relieved Riley hadn't told me or the others about her little visit to our creator. Victoria. This was the story she wanted the yellow-eyes to know—the story that didn't implicate Jane or the dark-cloaked Volturi. Well, I could play along. Hopefully the mind reader was already in the know.

I couldn't physically take revenge on this monster, but I could tell the yellow-eyes everything with my thoughts. I hoped.

I nodded, agreeing with Jane's little joke, and sat up because I wanted the mind reader's attention, whoever that was. I continued with the version of the story that any other member of my coven would have been able to give. I pretended I was Kevin. Dumb as a bag of rocks and totally ignorant.

"I don't know what happened." That part was

true. The mess on the battlefield was still a mystery. I'd never seen any of Kristie's group. Did the secret howler vampires get them? I would keep that secret for the yellow-eyes. "We split up, but the others never came. And Riley left us, and he didn't come to help like he promised. And then it was so confusing, and everybody was in pieces." I flinched at the memory of the torso I'd hurdled. "I was afraid. I wanted to run away." I nodded at Carlisle. "That one said they wouldn't hurt me if I stopped fighting."

This wasn't betraying Carlisle in any way. He'd already told Jane as much.

"Ah, but that wasn't his gift to offer, young one," Jane said. She sounded like she was enjoying herself. "Broken rules demand a consequence."

Still pretending I was Kevin, I just stared at her as if I were too stupid to understand.

Jane looked at Carlisle. "Are you sure you got all of them? The other half that split off?"

Carlisle nodded. "We split up, too."

So it *was* the howlers that got Kristie. I hoped that, whatever else they were, the howlers were really, really terrifying. Kristie deserved that.

"I can't deny that I'm impressed," Jane said, sounding sincere, and I thought that this was probably the truth. Jane had been hopeful that Victoria's army would do some damage here, and we'd clearly failed.

"Yes," the three vampires behind Jane all agreed quietly.

"I've never seen a coven escape this magnitude of offensive intact," Jane continued. "Do you know what was behind it? It seems like extreme behavior, considering the way you live here. And why was the girl the key?" Her eyes flicked to the human for just a moment.

"Victoria held a grudge against Bella," the red-head told her.

So the strategy finally made sense. Riley just wanted the girl dead and didn't care how many of us died to get it done.

Jane laughed happily. "This one"—and she smiled at the human the way she'd smiled at me—"seems to bring out bizarrely strong reactions in our kind."

Nothing happened to the girl. Maybe Jane didn't want to hurt her. Or maybe her horrible talent only worked on vampires.

"Would you please not do that?" the redhead asked in a controlled but furious voice.

Jane laughed again. "Just checking. No harm done, apparently."

I tried to keep my expression Kevin-ish and not betray my interest. So Jane couldn't hurt this girl the way she'd hurt me, and this was not a normal thing for Jane. Though Jane was laughing about it, I could tell it was driving her crazy. Was this why the human girl was tolerated by the yellow-eyes? But if she was special in some way, why didn't they just change her into a vampire?

"Well, it appears that there's not much left for us to do," Jane said, her voice a dead monotone again. "Odd. We're not used to being rendered unnecessary. It's too bad we missed the fight. It sounds like it would have been entertaining to watch."

"Yes," the redhead retorted. "And you were so close. It's a shame you didn't arrive just a half hour earlier. Perhaps then you could have fulfilled your purpose here."

I fought a smile. So the redhead was the mind reader, and he'd heard everything I'd wanted him to hear. Jane wasn't getting away with anything.

Jane stared back at the mind reader with a blank expression. "Yes. Quite a pity how things turned out, isn't it?"

The mind reader nodded, and I wondered what he was hearing in Jane's head.

Jane turned her blank face to me now. There was nothing in her eyes, but I could feel that my time had run out. She'd gotten what she needed from me. She didn't know that I'd also given the mind reader everything I could. And protected his coven's secrets, too. I owed him that. He'd punished Riley and Victoria for me.

I glanced at him from the corner of my eye and thought, *Thanks*.

"Felix?" Jane said lazily.

"Wait," the mind reader said loudly.

He turned to Carlisle and spoke quickly. "We could explain the rules to the young one. She doesn't seem unwilling to learn. She didn't know what she was doing."

"Of course," Carlisle said eagerly, looking at Jane. "We would certainly be prepared to take responsibility for Bree."

Jane's face looked like she wasn't sure if they were joking, but if they *were* joking, they were funnier than she'd given them credit for.

Me, I was touched to the core. These vampires were strangers, but they'd gone out on this dangerous limb for me. I already knew it wasn't going to work, but still.

"We don't make exceptions," Jane told them, amused. "And we don't give second chances. It's bad for our reputation."

It was like she was discussing someone else. I didn't care that she was talking about killing me. I knew the yellow-eyes couldn't stop her. She was the vampire police. But even though the vampire cops were dirty—really dirty—at least the yellow-eyes knew it now.

"Which reminds me . . . ," Jane went on, her eyes locking on the human girl again and her smile widening. "Caius will be *so* interested to hear that you're still human, Bella. Perhaps he'll decide to visit."

Still human. So they were going to change the girl. I wondered what they were waiting for.

"The date is set," said the little vampire with the short black hair and the clear voice. "Perhaps we'll come to visit you in a few months."

Jane's smile disappeared like someone had wiped it off. She shrugged without looking at the black-haired vampire, and I got the feeling that as much as she might have hated the human girl, she hated this small vampire ten times as much.

Jane turned back to Carlisle with the same vacant expression as before. "It was nice to meet you, Carlisle—I'd thought Aro was exaggerating. Well, until we meet again . . ."

This would be it, then. I still didn't feel afraid. My only regret was that I couldn't tell Fred more about all of this. He was going almost totally blind into this world full of dangerous politics and dirty cops and secret covens. But Fred was smart and careful and talented. What could they do to him if they couldn't even see him? Maybe the yellow-eyes would meet Fred someday. *Be nice to him, please*, I thought at the mind reader.

"Take care of that, Felix," Jane said indifferently, nodding at me. "I want to go home."

"Don't watch," the redheaded mind reader whispered.

I closed my eyes.